WILD AND WOUNDED

HONEYWELLS OF KENTUCKY, BOOK 2

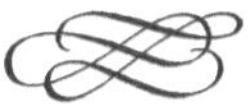

VANESSA GRAY BARTAL

DRY CREEK PRESS

Most twenty-year-old college juniors went to Florida for spring break, especially if they were men. Not so Corliss Honeywell. When he was with his brothers, he assumed the personality all of them shared—loud, boisterous, and rowdy. But on his own at college, he had discovered he was actually quiet and studious, preferring to stay at home and read on a Friday night instead of go out and party like everyone else on campus. If not for the fact that he was a starting forward on the basketball team, he might never leave his room at all, except to go to class. After so many years of living with five siblings, the solitude of college life was a fascinating new experience.

Not that he wasn't homesick, because he was. That was why, when his basketball team had missed the playoffs, he was elated. He wanted his team to win, but more than that, he wanted to go home to Kentucky for spring break. The only way he could do that was if he didn't have to play ball. He had pretended to be heartsick when the team lost the game that would take them to the playoffs, but in his heart he had been relieved.

Sometimes Corliss felt like he was two different people. As the second Honeywell son, he was as loud and rowdy as his brothers, he knew everything there was to know about horses, and enjoyed working with his hands. And then there was the other Corliss, the one no one knew, the one who attended college in Maine because he loved living on the ocean, the one who majored in English literature because he wanted to, the one who had memorized most of Charles Dickens' books.

Now that he was once again home in Kentucky, he was the Honeywell Corliss, the homogenized version of himself that was indistinguishable from his brothers. And the strange part was that he was okay with that. There was safety in numbers. He liked being part of a group, especially a group like his brothers. Together, they were an unstoppable force, sort of like a basketball team. They were certainly tall enough to be a basketball team; at 6'8", Corliss still only averaged somewhere in the middle.

"Mom and Dad got a new housekeeper," Grant announced when he picked him up from the airport.

"With only you and Ivy at home?" Corliss said. "I'm surprised." He, Brent, Darcy, and Everett were all at college, and Grant's turn would come next year after he graduated. Since Brent had taken a year off before going to school, he was also a junior. That meant their parents would have all five sons in five different colleges the following year.

"Mom says she doesn't see any of us ever leaving home," Grant said. "She says she might as well break in a new housekeeper gently while you're all away so she's prepared for you when you all return."

"That makes sense," Corliss said. He didn't see any of them going away, either. They loved their home, and there was room enough for all of them. Why go when staying was so very comfortable? "Are they local?" he asked, referring to the new housekeeper once again. Usually his parents culled someone from the area, but applicants were becoming fewer and farther between.

Grant shook his head. "They're from Ohio."

Corliss gasped. "Yankees?"

Grant nodded, his lips pressed together disapprovingly. Though Ohio was only a couple of hours away by car, it might as well have been another world in both custom and philosophy. How could their parents consider hiring someone who didn't know how to make sweet tea or had never heard of a hot-brown sandwich?

"She was the only one who applied," Grant continued. "And, get this, she

has a daughter. I haven't seen her yet. She's been staying with relatives while her mom gets settled in. She's Ivy's age, and she's coming this week."

Corliss smiled at the excitement in his brother's tone. The new girl would only be a year younger than Grant, four years younger than Corliss. He tried to imagine another Ivy in the house and frowned. Ivy was their baby and they all doted on her. She didn't need any competition for their affections. Good thing the new housekeeper had her own apartment over the office. At least the girl wouldn't actually be living in the house.

"Keep an eye on her," Corliss commanded. "I don't want Ivy picking up any Yankee ways." Perhaps the statement was ironic coming from someone who chose to attend college in the epicenter of Yankee territory, but he didn't care. He had no plans to adapt to a Yankee lifestyle, but Ivy was still impressionable. She might be wowed by their lack of accent and ability to eat a meal without cornbread.

"Oh, I'll keep an eye on her," Grant said enthusiastically.

Corliss looked out the window and smiled vaguely at the passing landscape. "What's her name?" he asked absently.

"The housekeeper is named Sandy. Her daughter is Allie."

Allie. Corliss repeated the name to himself a couple of times, wondering if it was short for something. Nice *name,* he thought.

If he had any idea of how the girl would change his life forever, he would have been more prepared to meet her.

CHAPTER 1

"Corliss!"

Corliss rolled his eyes and didn't answer. Everyone kept forgetting he couldn't yell in his current condition. Whoever it was would find him eventually, so he ignored them and kept busy working his horse. Behind him, a talk radio station spewed something about the current political climate. He reached over and switched it to a classical station.

His brother, Darcy, stepped into view. "There you are. I was yelling for you, but you didn't answer."

Corliss pointed to his jaw.

"Oh, right," Darcy said. "Can you come here a minute? I want you to look at this foot." He turned and walked to a neighboring barn, Corliss following obediently in his wake. Darcy gestured to the horse in question. Corliss stepped in and picked up the animal's hoof, turning it toward the light so he could see better. "What do you think? An abscess or thrush?"

Corliss plucked a tool from his belt and picked at the horse's hoof, scraping it and staring at what he had collected on the tool. "Thrush," he said irritably. As a farrier, he was in charge of all the horses' feet. He took it personally when something went wrong. He pulled a magnifying glass out of his tool belt and held it over the hoof. "There's a hole; he stepped on something." He set down the hoof, feeling slightly better. Clearly, the horse had stepped on something, allowing yeast to enter the wound and develop into thrush. That was a much better scenario than thrush by hoof neglect, something Corliss would never allow.

Darcy watched while his brother retrieved medicine from a shelf and rubbed it into the horse's wound. Then he picked up a piece of chalk and wrote on the slate outside the horse's stall, telling all who passed that the horse was out of commission until the thrush passed. With so many horses, the slate tablets were a handy way of communicating each horse's needs. No doubt everyone who saw the sign would stop to check on the horse and make sure he was doing okay, ensuring that his healing time would be as quick as possible.

"Sandy was upset this morning," Darcy said when Corliss was finished working.

Corliss clenched his jaw and winced, forgetting once again about his injury. "When isn't she upset?" he muttered. Since his jaw had been wired shut, he had been unable to speak clearly. Thankfully, his brothers had a sixth sense about what he was trying to say. Or they pretended to. Whatever the case, he never had to repeat himself with them.

"I don't think she was upset with you this time. I think she was really upset. Maybe…maybe something's up with Allie."

Corliss turned away, wincing again. The mention of Allie was as painful as his broken jaw. If something was wrong with Allie, he would never know; Sandy would make sure of it.

"Do you want me to try and find out?" Darcy asked.

Corliss shook his head.

"If something is wrong with Allie, you have the right to know," Darcy said.

"I have no rights when it comes to Allie," Corliss replied. "She's made that abundantly clear."

"Corliss, it's not right," Darcy said. "The whole situation isn't right."

"It is what it is, and I learned to accept it a long time ago," he lied. He would never accept the way things were between him and Allie, but he had no ability to fix them, either. He had never been able to impose his will on Allie, something else she made abundantly clear from their first meeting. "Did you need anything else before I return to my horse?"

"No, that was it. Thanks for the second opinion," Darcy said.

Corliss nodded. Since Darcy was an equine veterinarian, Corliss sincerely doubted he had needed a second opinion. The situation had probably been a ruse to discuss Sandy and Allie. He turned toward his barn and tried, unsuccessfully, to block out the painful memories, but they rose unbidden to the surface anyway. He reached the stall where he had previously been working and rested his forehead against the horse's neck. Sometimes he thought if he didn't have the comforting presence of the horses, he might truly lose his mind.

As if by magic, the familiar scent of sweet hay and pungent leather began to steal over him, calming his racing heart, easing his frayed emotions. Slowly, he opened his eyes and eased away from the horse. He wasn't any worse off today than he had been yesterday. He could survive another day. With that bolstering thought in mind, he picked up the horse's hoof and returned to work.

CHAPTER 2

No matter how hard he tried, Corliss couldn't sleep late on the farm. When he was at school, he could occasionally sleep past eight, but at home, he always woke at six. Today was no exception. He bounded outside to the horses and received a welcome greeting of whinnies. The familiar scent of the barn was as welcoming as the sound the horses were making. The briny scent of the ocean in Maine was pleasant, but nothing smelled like home.

He spent some time inspecting hooves as he walked through the horses' ranks, greeting each one individually with a pat on the neck. This summer he would begin his official training as a farrier. To some it might seem strange that he was majoring in literature when he already knew he was going to be a farrier, but fortunately for him, his parents believed strongly in education. They felt it made one an all around better person, even if it didn't have a direct impact on his career. And, who knew, maybe he would get his doctorate someday and teach some classes at the local college. The beauty of being a farrier was that it was a low-pressure job. He would have all the extra time and energy he wanted to devote to literary pursuits. Maybe he would even write that novel that had been tossing around in his mind for the last couple of years. Wouldn't that take everyone by surprise? A Honeywell who wrote a book.

By the time he finished inspecting the horses, it was late, much too late to eat breakfast with his family. He decided to grab a box of cereal in the kitchen. That way he would be able to eat the entire box in peace, without his mother lamenting his poor eating habits. She was a big believer in a full breakfast, but she always kept a dozen boxes of cereal on hand for her sons who seemingly had no end to their appetites.

As soon as he stepped into the kitchen, he saw her. She was bent over the kitchen island, reading a book. He would have backed out, preferring not to interrupt her or interact with a stranger, but she noticed him as soon as he took a step into the room. She put down her book and gave him such an inviting smile that he found himself smiling in return.

"I came for cereal," he announced, as if he needed a reason to enter his own kitchen.

"Don't expect me to get it for you," she said. "I don't work for you." She rested her chin in her hand and studied him as he took out the cereal, a giant bowl, spoon, and milk.

"Are you sure you don't want a bigger bowl?" she asked. "We could try to find you a satellite dish."

He smiled, surprised by her plucky attitude. Most local girls ducked and covered when they saw him and his brothers coming. "You must be Allie," he said.

"If I must, then I guess I am." He sat across from her at the island and tried to eat, despite the fact that she was still staring at him. She straightened, clasped her hands behind her back, and began to prowl around him, inspecting him as if she were trying to decide whether or not to purchase him.

"Are you going to kick my tires?" he asked.

"I wouldn't want to break my foot," she replied. She came to a stop beside him. "So you're one of the famous Honeywells."

"Famous?"

"Infamous, really. Yesterday I went to town, and not only did everyone immediately know I was new, but they knew I was living here. I was warned not to turn my back on any of you." She narrowed her eyes and inspected him from head to toe again. "I think they were exaggerating. You're not so scary. Cute, but not scary."

He laughed. "Aren't you sixteen?"

"Last time I checked," she said.

"I'm twenty. That's too old for you."

She hopped onto the stool beside him and crossed her legs, resting her clasped hands on her knee. "Did I say I was interested? Besides, I happen to think twenty is too young for me. If I'm really going to commit to being a gold digger, then I need to set my sights on someone who doesn't have to share his wealth with five siblings, someone who is closer to death than twenty." She paused. "Do you know any ninety-year-olds in poor health who are looking for a wife?"

"Are you sure you want to be a gold digger? There are easier ways to make money."

"Yes, but none more respectable. I want the panache of being that girl who preys on the weak and innocent, using my wiles to charm helpless old men out of their fortunes."

"Dare to dream big," he said.

"Exactly." She hopped off the stool and collected her book. She was like a live wire, moving and talking with constant energy. Corliss couldn't be sure, but he thought she was sparkling somehow. And she was pretty. Her long brown hair was swept up into a ponytail that twitched whenever she moved. And since she was always moving, it twitched constantly, like the tail of a cat who was about to pounce.

He reached across the island, tipping her book down so he could read the title. "You're a fan of Henry James?" he asked.

"I don't know. This is the first book of his I've read, but so far so good." Her tone was wary, and he sensed she was sensitive about enjoying literature.

He smiled. "I have his entire collection if you care to read more."

One of her perfectly manicured eyebrows arched in surprise. "What's your name?"

"Corliss," he said.

"Corliss, you're looking better and better to me. If only you were ninety." With that, she swept from the room, leaving him chuckling in her wake.

Later that day, he heard her on the piano. He knew it was her because no one else played it. She looked up self-consciously when he entered the room and paused from trying to pluck out a song.

"I've always wanted to learn to play," she said. By her caught, guilty expression he wondered if she thought maybe she was in trouble for touching the beautiful grand piano. He walked to the piano, leaned over her, and played a short Chopin prelude.

"I could teach you, if you want," he said. He winked at her and left the room, smiling when she stared after him in surprise.

When he ran into her a third time that day, he wasn't sure it was an accident. But how could she have known which hayloft was his favorite reading spot? Apparently she had also decided it was a good spot for reading because she was curled up with her book. She didn't look up when he approached, but she did speak.

"Stalking is a crime in all fifty states," she said.

"I'm glad to hear you say that," he said, sitting down beside her and taking out his own book. "I was beginning to fear you had an obsessive crush on me."

"Not obsessive," she said in the same casual tone.

He smiled and leaned back. Opening his book, he almost forgot her completely when she spoke again. "What are you reading?" she whispered.

He closed his book to show her the cover. She whistled appreciatively. "Beowulf. That's heavy."

"I have a paper due on it when I return next week," he said.

"If you need any help, let me know," she said.

He laughed. "I might do that. Something tells me you could write a good paper with lots of mindless filler. That's the kind of stuff professors like."

"That's why I'll make a good lawyer; I can talk a long time without saying anything at all."

He closed his book again and turned to study her. "You want to be a lawyer?"

She closed her book and looked up at him. "Yes," she said, sounding almost shy for the first time.

"That's not fair," he said.

"What's not fair?"

"Smart and pretty—a killer combination."

Her lashes fluttered in surprise. "Corliss, you're my favorite brother."

"Have you met any of the others?" he asked.

"No, but I have a feeling things won't change."

He smiled, but he had a feeling things were about to change completely. And when she resumed reading her book and rested her head lightly on his shoulder, he was certain he was right.

CHAPTER 3

$\mathcal{C}$orliss finished his work and lingered in the barn, avoiding the painful memories of the house. Not that the barn wasn't rife with painful memories, because it was. In fact, there was no part of the farm that hadn't been touched by Allie's lively presence, but at least all the memories that happened here were innocent. All the ugliness had taken place somewhere else, somewhere far away. Unfortunately for Corliss, nowhere was far enough to escape the pain of his gaping emotional wounds.

He plodded toward the house, pausing on the front porch to remove his boots. The four other pairs of wellies already lined up told him his brothers had beaten him home. He slipped his shoes between those belonging to Brent and Darcy. Since all the boots looked exactly alike, they always kept them in age order.

He entered the nearest bathroom and spent a long time cleaning up, vigorously scrubbing his nails with a brush. Even that action was a painful reminder of Allie. How many times had she stood in the doorway and watched, teasing him for his fastidiousness.

"It's supper, Corliss, not brain surgery. You can leave some germs behind."

How many times had he picked her up and carried her to the

supper table, tucked under one arm like a football while she laughed and tried to wriggle free?

When he could put it off no longer, Corliss left the bathroom and walked slowly toward the dining room. Sandy glanced at him with her usual scowl before marching out of the room. Supper was already in progress, so Corliss retrieved his own food. Mashing it into oblivion with his fork, he gently shoved it between the wires of his mouth, trying to swallow without chewing.

For five years, Sandy had been treating him like public enemy number one. In the beginning, his parents had offered to fire her, but Corliss refused. Sandy needed the job, he'd said. The truth was that she was his only remaining connection to Allie. But maybe it was time to let her go. Her anger only added to his misery, and he already had more than he could handle.

Supper was an oddly silent affair, and Corliss wondered why. Usually his brothers argued about one inane topic or another. He usually joined in, especially if it was a really stupid debate. There was nothing like arguing the pros and cons of honey versus maple syrup to take his mind off his troubles. But tonight there was no ridiculous topic to take his mind off things. Instead he ate in silence, trying to stuff the mush in his mouth as quickly as possible so he could flee to his room and lose himself in a good book.

"Corliss, can we talk to you? In the den," his mother said, casting a furtive look toward the kitchen.

Corliss followed his parents to the den and sat in the recliner, waiting. He tried to remember the last time his parents asked to have a serious talk with him. It had been about five years ago, and it had concerned Allie, but that couldn't be today's topic, could it? Why would they mention Allie out of the blue?

His parents sat on the couch and clasped hands. "Sandy is upset today," his mother said.

"That's no different than any other day," Corliss interrupted.

"Today was different," his father said. "She wasn't angry; she was crying. She didn't want to tell us, but we finally pried it out of her. It's Allie."

Corliss's heart squeezed. "What about Allie?"

"I don't know. All she would say is that she's worried about Allie. I think she's in some kind of trouble or danger."

Danger? Allie was in danger? He shot to his feet. "I'm going. Darcy can handle the trimming until I get back, although everything is in good shape."

His mother took a deep breath. "Corliss, are you sure this is a good idea? I mean, you and Allie haven't spoken in five years. After you came home last time, you were so…I don't want to see you like that again. I don't want things to be worse than they are now."

"Then why did you tell me?" he asked.

"Because you have a right to know," his father said.

Corliss nodded. "And I also have a right to go. I'll be back when I'm sure she's out of danger." He pivoted around the coffee table and strode to the kitchen. Sandy looked up with a smile until she realized it was him.

"Where is she?" he blurted.

"What's it to you?" she said.

"Don't play games, Sandy. You told Mom and Dad she's in trouble, and I'm going. I need to know where she is."

Sandy pressed her lips together and shook her head. Corliss took a step forward until he towered over her. He couldn't remember the last time he had been so livid. "Is she in danger?"

She looked away, not meeting his eyes, but the telltale quiver of her lips was all the answer he needed.

"No matter what's passed between us, do you think I would ever let anything happen to her? I would die first, and you know it. Now where is she?"

Sandy swallowed hard and squeezed her eyes tightly shut. "She's in the same place. She never left."

She hadn't left? That was…unexpected. Corliss took an uncertain step back.

Sandy used the opportunity to advance on him, her hands on her hips. "Don't you hurt her, Corliss Honeywell. Do you hear me? If your hurt my little girl again, don't bother coming back here, or

I'm leaving." For emphasis, she jabbed her finger hard against his chest.

With a sigh, he clasped her wrist and pried her finger from his chest. "Someday maybe Allie will tell you the truth of what really happened, Sandy. Until then, you'd do best to keep your opinions to yourself."

She blinked at him in shock. It was the first time he had ever commented on the subject. She swallowed hard, looking away. "Take care of her, Corliss. Please," she practically choked on the word, but at least she had added it. That was a step up.

"You know I will," he said.

He packed with haste, belatedly remembering to ask one of his brothers to drive him to the airport. Instead of one, they all came, driving silently in a full-force show of support. He knew if they could, they would all come with him. He wished they could. With them, he knew who he was, he knew where he stood. Alone, he wasn't so sure, and that was how he would have to face Allie—uncertain, defenseless, alone.

They walked him to his gate, and Brent finally spoke. "All you have to do is call," he said. "We'll all be there."

Corliss nodded.

They waited in continued silence until the last possible moment, until his plane took off. Most people underestimated the strength of the bond between the brothers. They might fight with everyone else, but they never fought with each other. They were there for each other, always, and they didn't like to be apart. If not for Allie, Corliss wouldn't be leaving now. He hated the adrift feeling he got whenever he was on his own. Being a Honeywell was part of his identity. On his own, he wasn't certain he much cared for Corliss. As a Honeywell, he was capable and in control. As Corliss, he had lost the only thing that ever meant anything to him.

As soon as he was on the plane, he took out his book and read *Oliver Twist,* but, like everything else, that soon brought a memory of Allie he was unable to suppress. Because he had nothing better to do, he let it play, enjoying the bittersweet twist of pain it caused.

CHAPTER 4

Corliss walked across the stage. With one hand he accepted his diploma. With the other, he transferred his tassel from one side to the other. In the audience, his family screamed so wildly that the faculty lining the stage turned to look with disapproving frowns. All of them were there, except Brent, who would be graduating himself in less than a week. Corliss squinted, trying to see her, trying to see Allie.

She was his graduation present, and he couldn't wait to see her. His parents had tried to talk him out of inviting her, but he wouldn't be dissuaded. The trip was as much for her as it was for him. Allie dreamed of traveling, of being anywhere but Kentucky. She had searched his pictures and begged him for stories of Maine so many times it would have been cruel not to bring her along. Besides, he wanted her there. She was as much a part of him as his family.

The spotlight was too bright to see his family, even though he knew the general area they were sitting. He sat impatiently through the remainder of the ceremony, then stood and dutifully threw his cap into the air with his classmates. At long last, the recessional began to play and he was almost free. He burst through the double doors leading outside and turned to wait; he didn't have to wait long.

"Corliss!" Even above the din of conversation swirling around him, he

had no trouble hearing Allie when she yelled. He was thankful for his height, which allowed him to see over heads without standing on his toes. She ran through the doors, a good ten paces ahead of his family. She sprinted toward him, arms outstretched. He bent and picked her up, holding her close and turning her in a circle.

She clasped his neck tightly, pressing her cheek to his. "I'm so proud," she whispered near his ear. "You're going to be the most educated farrier the world has ever known."

He laughed. "Can't you give me a break, Allie? Not even on my graduation day?"

He set her down and she clasped his hands. "Did I say a word about you wasting your potential? Did I mention that you're brilliant and you're going to spend your life trimming hooves? No, I didn't say a word."

"Thanks for not bringing it up on this most momentous of days," he said dryly, letting go of one of her hands and slinging his arm over her shoulders. His family reached them, but he didn't let Allie go as he hugged his parents.

His brothers stood scanning the crowd with their usual expression of "What trouble can we get into?" Their mother caught the look and preempted them. "Don't even think about it. We're leaving right after supper to go to Washington. If any of you does anything to get detained in Maine and we miss Brent's baccalaureate, you're going to get it."

The brothers frowned, but they didn't argue. If there was one person in the world they feared, it was their mother.

"We could stay with Corliss and Allie. We could go tomorrow," Grant suggested.

Their mother's gaze narrowed. "No. I'm not taking any chances on leaving you alone here. You're all going with me, and I don't want to hear another word."

"Yes, ma'am," they said in unison, as if they were still ten years old and not grown men.

"I wish you and Allie were coming tonight, too, Corliss." His mother turned her worried expression on him. She hadn't liked the idea of leaving Allie with him, and neither had Sandy. Despite his assurances that she would be okay, he didn't think it was her physical safety they were worried about.

"It's really going to be okay, Mom," he said. "Besides, I promised to show Allie the sights. She's never seen the ocean before."

Allie bobbed up and down excitedly, wisely remaining silent for once. Consent had already begrudgingly been given for her stay. No need to take the chance of having it revoked.

They went to a lobster pound for supper. Because it was spring and not lobster season, they had to drive for a while to find an open pound. But not only was it an authentic Maine experience, it was the most expedient way to feed their large brood. Plus, they could eat outdoors, which meant they could talk as loudly as they wanted with no disapproving looks from the wait staff or other customers. Of course that didn't stop the disapproving looks from their mother as she repeatedly reminded them to use good table manners.

While his mother worked on their manners, Corliss repeatedly reminded Allie to eat. She was enthralled with the ocean, watching the powerful waves crash against the large rocks that jutted the shore. Absently, she rested her hand on his leg and he covered it with his hand.

"Allie, you're freezing. I told you to dress warmly. It's colder here in May than it is in Kentucky."

"I didn't want to layer up," she said vaguely, still staring at the ocean.

"Why not?"

"Because I look cuter in summer clothes. No one looks cute in a parka."

He rolled his eyes. "I already know you're cute. What do you care what anyone else thinks?"

"Do you think we'll see a whale?" she asked, squinting at the horizon.

"I'm positive we will," he assured her. "Now finish your food, please. Between the chill and lack of sustenance, you're going to keel over like a character in a Jane Austen novel."

She turned to smile at him then. "That only happened when her characters were lovesick. But I have no reason to be lovesick, do I, Corliss?" She batted her lashes at him.

"Eat your food," he said, deftly dodging the subject.

"It's so beautiful here," Ivy said. "Maybe I'll go to college here."

"No," the brothers answered in unison.

She rolled her eyes and returned to her food in silence.

"I thought she's going to the University of Kentucky," Allie whispered.

"She is, but she keeps trying to get away. I don't know why," Corliss answered, frowning at the top of Ivy's head. Beside him, Allie chuckled silently to herself. "What?" he asked.

"Nothing," she said. Then her smile changed to a frown. "Corliss, how come you didn't try to talk me into going to college closer to home?"

"Because you're not my sister," he said, cracking open a lobster claw.

She faced forward with another frown.

"What?" he asked, nudging her leg with his.

"Nothing," she said. Her listless tone told him that nothing meant something, but they had two days together; he would pry it out of her eventually.

After supper, they said goodbyes to his family. Corliss blushed when his mother pulled him aside and whispered in his ear. "She's eighteen and the housekeeper's daughter, Corliss. Don't you dare do anything I'll regret."

His sneaky mother made sure and emphasized that she might regret something he wouldn't give a second thought to. He promised to be good, and she relaxed slightly before hugging Allie goodbye and waving to them both. He and Allie stood arm in arm, waving them away. When they were out of sight, Allie looked up at him with a mischievous smile. "Now what?"

"Now we see your whales. Come on, we have to hurry." He clasped her hand and dragged her behind him, jogging to the end of a long pier. As if by magic, a boat appeared and helped them embark. Corliss took off his jacket and wrapped it around Allie, then put his arm around her waist and held her close, swallowing her whole in his embrace. She wrapped her arms around his waist and they stood swaying together as the boat took off toward the ocean. The swirling, tearing wind made conversation impossible, but that was okay. The scene was breathtaking enough to leave them speechless anyway.

When they came upon a pod of whales, the engine cut and idled as they drifted closer and closer to the whales. It only took Corliss a moment to realize Allie was crying. Since he had rarely seen her cry in the two years he'd known her, he was immediately concerned.

"These are happy tears," she explained, swiping at her eyes. "I never dreamed I would experience something like this, Corliss. Thank you." She beamed up at him before quickly returning her attention to the whales.

After the whales went away, they continued, seeing puffins, dolphins, *seals, otters, and an eagle. Allie was shimmering with excitement when they returned to the shore.*

"Why were we the only people on the boat?" she asked suspiciously.

"Because it's not tourist season yet. The boats aren't in regular operation. I chartered it special," Corliss answered.

"Corliss," Allie exclaimed. "That must have cost a fortune."

"It wasn't that much," Corliss assured her. "And who cares if it was? This is your once-in-a-lifetime adventure, Allie. What's money compared to your happiness?"

She frowned and bit her lip. "Sometimes I hate that you have money. It makes it so hard to buy for you."

He slipped his arm around her shoulders as they walked down the pier. "You bought something for me?"

"Duh, Corliss, it's your graduation. Of course I bought you a present."

He grinned. "What is it?"

"It's in the car," she said excitedly. She grasped his hand and started to jog toward the car. Since his legs were so much longer, he easily overtook her, then he picked her up, tossing her onto his back without breaking stride—a move they had perfected over the years. They reached the car and she slid down from his back.

"Can we sit inside?" she asked. "I'm freezing. You should have warned me it was colder here." She gave him a cheeky grin and dodged him when he reached to pinch her waist. He opened her door and closed it after she was safely inside.

He slid behind the steering wheel and started the car, blasting the heat on high until the car warmed up. "Where is my present, kid?" he asked.

She reached under the seat and handed him a neatly wrapped rectangle. "I wanted to buy you a first edition or an autographed copy, but I didn't have an extra two hundred thousand dollars lying around. Instead I bought you the best one I could find, and I hope the sentimental value will make it more worthwhile to you."

He opened the box to reveal a leather-bound edition of his favorite book, Oliver Twist. "I love it," he said sincerely, tracing his finger lightly over the gold edging. "Thanks, Allie." He leaned over the console to place a kiss on her cheek, but she turned her head, trying vainly to capture his lips. He eased away and pressed his back against the door.

"What are you doing?" he asked, wary now.

"Trying to kiss you," she said. "I thought it was obvious."

"It was obvious what you were doing, but not why," he said.

She rolled her eyes. "You said we could be together when I was older, Corliss. I'm eighteen now. I'll graduate high school in a month. You graduated college, and you're coming home. This seems an ideal time."

He shook his head. "Eighteen is still too young, Allie. What about college? Or have you forgotten Chicago?"

She stuck out her bottom lip in a pout and crossed her arms over her chest. "Why do you keep putting me off? I'm beginning to think you don't love me at all."

Corliss set the book aside and reached for her, dragging her over the console to sit in his lap. "Allie, don't be crazy. You know I love you. But now is not the right time for us. I know what college is like. You're about to spread your wings and be independent. I don't want you to be tied down to some old guy from home. I want you to be free to have all the experiences college has to offer without a jealous boyfriend hanging over your shoulder. Can't you understand?"

"I suppose," she said sullenly. "But why won't you at least kiss me? You've never kissed me, Corliss, even though I've practically gift-wrapped myself for you."

He smiled and smoothed a wayward strand of hair off her face. "Because, Allie, when I kiss you, I have no intention of stopping. Once won't ever be enough." He pressed a kiss to her forehead and held her tightly as they watched the sun go down from the warm shelter of his car.

CHAPTER 5

The first thing Corliss did when he exited the plane in Chicago was try to buy a gun. At home, he and his brothers had enough guns to form an arsenal, but he wasn't so stupid that he didn't realize he couldn't exactly sneak a gun onto an airplane, to say nothing of taking it across state lines. He knew large cities like Chicago had stricter gun laws than other places, and he intended to find out what they were.

He found the first reputable-looking gun store he ran across and stopped in to register for a weapon. There was the requisite three day waiting period, then he would have to apply for a concealed-carry permit, take a class, and register his weapon with the Chicago police department.

"Why do y'all have to do that?" he asked the store owner.

"They say it's so they'll know who has guns when they show up at houses. Personally, I think it's Big Brother sticking his finger into our business."

Corliss didn't disagree, but this wasn't his city. He would do what he needed to in order to keep Allie safe, and if that meant jumping over legal barrels, then so be it. In the mean time while he waited for his gun, he bought ammunition, a wicked looking knife, a stun gun, and a can of pepper spray. The last two items were for Allie, if he could get her to carry them.

Buying something for Allie felt strangely intimate, even if it was a weapon. He distracted himself by getting the number of someone who could teach a concealed carry class for him.

"I'll give you the number, but they're full up," the clerk said. "Lots of people want guns these days."

"I think I'll be able to convince him to work me in," Corliss said confidently. He took the number, stepped out of the store, and called the man who ran the classes. A thousand dollars later, the man agreed to see him the next day for a private class.

Corliss checked his watch. Because of the time difference, he would still be able to catch Allie at work. That was probably for the best. Lots of witnesses might keep her from making a scene. He hailed a cab downtown, trying to suppress the ever-present memories that refused to leave him alone. He hadn't set foot in Chicago in five years; he shouldn't still know it like the back of his hand. He shouldn't be able to look on almost every corner and remember a scene with Allie as the star.

The taxi dropped him in front of the courthouse. He couldn't escape a moment of pride that she had succeeded. The cost had been high, but she had done what she had set out to do, becoming a prosecutor in one of the largest cities in the United States.

Before heading to the courthouse, he walked down the street to the bus station and stuffed his belongings in a locker. He wasn't anxious to explain to court security why he was armed with a knife, pepper spray, and stun gun. A quick glance at the directory in the lobby showed him Allie's floor. He rode the elevator, taking note as he did so how easy it was to get to her. After exiting the elevator, he headed to an overworked and harassed-looking secretary, asked for Allie, and was directed to her cubicle. There were several prosecutors in her office, and none was important enough yet for a real office. Allie's cubicle was in the middle. Corliss's heart thumped hard in his chest, but needlessly so because when he rounded the corner she wasn't there.

"You looking for Allison?" A pretty woman with a nice smile spoke from the next cubicle.

"Yes," he said, as politely as he could with his jaw still clenched tightly shut. She looked taken aback by the firm set of his lips. He pointed to his face. "Sorry, I have a broken jaw. It's a real hassle. You were telling me where I could find Allie?"

"Hmm, oh, right, Allie." She tore her eyes from his jaw and looked in his eyes again. Apparently she approved of whatever she read there because she smiled again. "She's in court today. She's probably about finished up now. If you hurry, you can catch her."

He nodded. "Thank you." He felt her eyes on him as he walked away. Were she and Allie friends? Had Allie told her about him? Had she told anyone? Probably not. He wouldn't tell anyone about her, but everyone already knew.

He jogged next door to the courthouse, stopping only to ask directions from another harried-looking clerk. The man directed him to Allie with a jerk of his head and a point of his finger before returning to his phone call.

This time there was no stopping the frantic beating of Corliss's heart. He skipped the elevator and ran up three flights of stairs, but the exertion did nothing to calm him. He tried to take a few deep breaths, but it wasn't easy with his mouth wired shut. Sucking air through his nose didn't provide the same calming effect as gulping oxygen with his mouth.

When he reached her courtroom, he inched the door open, peeking inside the quiet room. Allie stood at the front, pacing in front of the jury box, talking to the man on the witness stand. Corliss eased into the room and sat in the back row, listening.

Before he could absorb any of what she was saying, he had to wrap his mind around her appearance. She didn't look like his Allie. Her hair was long again and secured severely on the back of her head. He supposed it made her look more lawyerly, but it didn't suit her personality. Or maybe it did now because gone was the sparkle, sunshine, and sass he had always associated with her. She looked thinner, too, as if she hadn't been eating properly, and she wore square-framed glasses. Corliss suspected those were also for effect, to make her look smarter, because she had perfect vision.

Her suit was well cut and flattered her slim figure, but he didn't like it. He wanted to see her in the soft, flowing dresses she had always preferred. He had always associated Allie with sunflowers and summertime because she loved to wear sundresses in the summer. Even in winter, he'd had a difficult time trying to keep her layered up. He smiled, thinking how much she hated to wear a coat. He wondered if she wore one now.

What do I need a coat for, Corliss? I have you, and you have enough body heat for both of us.

But what about the times when I'm not with you, he would say.

I'll store up all my shivers and save them for you, was her standard reply. Then she would burrow herself into his embrace, pressing her lips to his neck so that he was usually the one who shivered.

He swallowed hard, pushing away the memory, wishing he could purge them from his mind so they would stop torturing him. But there were so many good times between them, how could he help but remember?

Finally, he forced his focus to Allie and the man on the stand who was squirming. He smiled, listening to Allie's fiery examination with interest.

"Mr. Pratt, is it fair to say you and your wife were not on the best of terms?" she asked.

"We fought like all couples do," the man answered uncomfortably.

"Not all couples have the police called on them over a dozen times in one year."

"Objection." The defense attorney shot to his feet. "Your honor, is there a question in the counselor's statement?"

"He has a point, counselor," the judge said. "Get to yours."

"People's evidence C342 shows a call log listing twelve police complaints filed by your neighbors. Of those twelve calls, how many times were you arrested, Mr. Pratt?"

He cleared his throat. "I don't remember."

"The number is eight times, isn't it, sir?"

"Could be."

"Should I bring out the record of those arrests to refresh your memory? I have all eight right here." She waved a sheaf of papers in the air.

"All right, it was eight times, but..."

She interrupted before he could continue. "And of those eight arrests, how many resulted in a domestic violence charge?"

"I don't rem..."

"Let me prompt your faulty memory. Of those eight arrests, all eight resulted in charges for domestic violence, didn't they, Mr. Pratt?"

"I suppose."

"And of those eight charges, how many were dropped? Isn't it true that six of those charges are still pending because all six happened in the past four months before your wife's disappearance?"

"Well, I..."

"And isn't it true that on the night before your wife disappeared from your home, the police were called to your residence?"

"Well, yes, but..."

"And when the police arrived, you told them your wife had gone out, is that correct, sir?"

"Yes, and..."

"But your neighbor, Mrs. Carlisle, the one who made the complaint, has already testified that she was watching your residence as she waited for the police to arrive. How do you explain the fact that she didn't see your wife leave your house?"

There was no time for Corliss to react when Mr. Pratt erupted from the defense box and leapt at Allie. Fortunately, the bailiff had apparently anticipated the act. Corliss hoped that didn't mean it happened to her often. In any case, he tackled the man, snagging his arms behind his back until he was subdued. The defense attorney rose and, with a sigh, requested a recess until after the weekend.

The judge granted his request and Allie turned toward her seat. She didn't smile, but Corliss could tell she was pleased. He would have grimaced if his face was able to perform the action. She was pleased a man had tried to attack her. What was wrong with her?

Court was adjourned and Allie stood. Corliss remained seated. His large size would draw attention, and he wanted to observe her awhile longer before making his presence known.

Later, he wished he had stood and revealed himself because it might have stopped him from witnessing what he saw next. A man who had been sitting in the front row stood. Allie turned, a friendly smile on her face. The man leaned forward and whispered in her ear. Her smile widened and she nodded. Corliss watched, tight-fisted, as the man's hand snaked up to land on her elbow, giving it a squeeze. He couldn't be sure what happened after that because suddenly he was seeing everything through a foggy red haze. He stood. People around him cleared a path, making him wonder what his expression looked like. In three steps, he was in front of Allie, and his mind was a total blank as he stared at her, waiting for her to notice him.

CHAPTER 6

*C*orliss couldn't stop smiling as he watched the top of Allie's square hat. Unlike his small college, there were too many in her graduating class to parade across the stage. Still, he couldn't be prouder, even if he didn't get to physically see her receive her diploma. Magna cum laude was an accomplishment for anyone, but when someone worked as hard as Allie worked to put herself through school and still was able to graduate with honors, well, the odds had been against her, to say the least.

The audience was so large Corliss was afraid to blink, lest he somehow lose her. He approached her while her back was turned. She stood in a circle of her friends, laughing and talking happily, using her hands to express her every emotion. She was still his live wire, still the sparkle in his day. Her friends spotted him and stopped talking, their mouths going slack with surprise.

"Uh, Allie," one of them said.

Allie stiffened and spun, all traces of humor clearing from her expression. "Mr. Honeywell," she said coolly.

"Ah, Allie, come on. You can't still be mad at me," he said.

"I can, and I am."

"I came all the way from Kentucky to see you," he said.

"Uninvited," she said.

Her mother came up beside them then. "Allie," she snapped. "That's rude."

"Mom, you always take his side," Allie said.

"That's because I'm always right," Corliss added with a grin.

Allie glared at him.

Sandy turned to Corliss. "Come out and eat with us, Corliss. Then you and Allie can drop me at the hotel and have a chance to talk."

"Mom," Allie intoned.

"He came all this way to see you, Allie," her mother said.

"Yeah, I came all this way to see you, Allie," Corliss echoed.

"I'm going out with my friends after we eat," she said with another quelling glare at Corliss.

"Super. I'll tag along. I'm dying to meet your friends." They were still standing behind Allie, hanging on every word. He shot them his most charming smile and they chorused their agreement to his proposal.

"Guys," Allie said, turning to frown at them.

"What?" One of them said. "We've been dying to meet him for years."

Corliss's smile increased while Allie's scowl deepened. "Let's get this over with. I'll meet up with you guys later." She waved to her friends and stalked off, Corliss and her mother chatting while they trailed slowly in her wake.

Allie led them to her favorite mother-appropriate restaurant, a stuffed-crust pizza place a few blocks off Michigan Avenue. Corliss sat beside her, draping his arm on the back of her chair. When she tried to scoot away, he wouldn't let her. Her mother looked on with a benevolent smile, inching Allie's irritation up even further.

She sat back, letting Corliss and her mother carry the conversation over dinner. They both seemed equally amused, as if Allie were a toddler having a tantrum and would soon forget it. But she wouldn't; she had promised herself that she would never forgive Corliss, no matter how charming and handsome he might be. Of course, she hadn't taken physical touch into account when she made her vow. Corliss began playing gently with the ends of her hair, softening her resolve. He knew she loved to have her hair played with; it was the one physical touch he had always indulged in with her.

The thought of how reserved he had otherwise been made her remember why she was so mad at him in the first place. She shook her head, tugging her hair from his reach. But instead of taking the hint, he dropped his hand to her knee and gave it a gentle squeeze.

Fine, he could touch her, but she didn't have to respond to him. It was a gentle touch on her knee. No big deal. But when her mother excused herself to use the restroom, he leaned forward and kissed her earlobe.

"You're cute when you're angry. I've missed you like crazy." He straightened up as her mother returned, pretending he hadn't said a word. The words lingered with Allie, though, softening her when she tried to steel herself against him.

By the time they deposited her mother at her hotel, she didn't shrug away from him when he rested his arm on her shoulders. She still didn't talk to him, though. They reached the club where she was meeting her friends, and she looked at Corliss, biting her lip. The club scene wasn't exactly his type of place, but he smiled and took her hand, leading her forward as if he owned the place.

He introduced himself to her friends, putting forth his most charming demeanor. They oohed and aahed over his sweet southern accent, his height, his dark good looks, and description of his family home. They plied him with questions about his relationship with Allie, which he answered with aplomb, making it appear as if he and Allie were some type of star-crossed lovers who were finally allowed to be together.

Allie frowned. Was that how he saw her? Did he think she was all wrong for him or out of reach? He had never mentioned the fact that she was the housekeeper's daughter, but did he think about it? Did that explain his reluctance to be with her?

"C'mere," Corliss said. She trailed behind him absently, not realizing until he took her in his arms that they were on the dance floor. They danced in silence for a couple minutes as Corliss held her close and studied her somber expression.

"Allie, don't be mad at me," he whispered. "It's been five months. I didn't know you were coming home for Christmas break."

"You were on a date, Corliss," she said, unable to hold back the words anymore. "With another girl," she added for emphasis.

"It was only a date," he said. "It didn't mean anything. I didn't ask her,

she asked me because she needed an escort to her parents' soiree. That was the only time I've ever seen her."

"Have there been other dates the last four years?" she asked.

His lack of answer was all the answer she needed. She tried to worm away, but he pinned her to his chest.

"Did you go on dates?" he asked. "Were there other men?"

"Yes there were other men," she tossed out, then backpedaled when he winced. "You told me to date other men, remember?"

"Yes, I remember. I was trying to do what was best for you, what was best for both of us. But I'm done with that. You're out of college, and I can't wait any longer."

Her heart thrummed, but she wasn't ready to let him off the hook so easily. "So because I've reached the magic number in your head, you're ready to be together. And I'm supposed to jump on board, just like that."

He nodded.

"It doesn't work that way," she said peevishly. "I'm staying in Chicago for law school. I'm not coming back to Kentucky."

"So?"

She blinked at him. She had expected him to argue with her. "What do you mean 'so?' Is that all you have to say when I tell you I'm not coming home?"

"I never expected you to come home," he said. "There are no law schools there. We'll be together long distance until you're finished."

She wracked her brain, trying to think up more excuses not to be together. "You've put me off for so long, I'm not sure I'm ready to forgive you so easily."

He smiled. "I was hoping you might say that."

"You were?" she asked, dumbfounded by his ready agreement tonight.

He nodded. "I have a really great way to make it up to you." He bent and kissed her, lightly at first, then with a blazing intensity totally inappropriate for their very public setting.

"That's possibly the most intense first kiss I've ever had," Allie said when they finally broke apart.

Corliss smiled. "It's been building for six years. And do you remember what I told you, Allie? There's no stopping with one." Before she could reply, he bent and kissed her again.

CHAPTER 7

*A*llie looked up with a smile that soon faded. She paled and swayed, leaning heavily on the man standing next to her. He looked up at Corliss with a frown.

"Allison, are you okay?" the man asked, his tone solicitous. When she didn't answer, he looked at Corliss again. "Sir, I'm going to have to ask you to back up."

Corliss ignored him and took a step closer, trying desperately to think of something to say.

"Sir," the man said with more force. He moved aside his coat to reveal a gun and a badge. "Step away from Miss Miller, or I'll have to use force."

"Honeywell," Corliss murmured.

The man frowned. "What?"

"Her name's not Miller, it's Honeywell."

Now the man looked questioningly at Allie. "Do you know this guy, Allison?"

Allie didn't answer, but Corliss did. "Of course she does. She's my wife. Happy anniversary, Allie. What do you get for the five year mark? Is it paper? Because I never received any divorce papers from you. Did they get lost in the mail?"

"Stop," Allie choked. She whipped off her glasses, pressing her hand over her eyes. She took a deep breath and stood straighter, easing away from the other man. "Stop this, Corliss. Go home." She tried to ease past him, but of course she couldn't.

"No," he said.

She stopped short and glared at him. "What?"

"You heard me. I'm not leaving."

She crossed her arms protectively over her chest, striking a defensive pose. "If you came here to serve me divorce papers, then you could have had them delivered."

"I'm not here to serve papers. I'm here to…" He trailed off, feeling ridiculous having this conversation in front of the strange man who was most likely her boyfriend. "Do you mind?" he snapped.

Allie sighed. "You can go, Marlin. Thank you."

"Are you sure, Allison?" the guy asked uneasily. "I don't like the looks of this guy."

Corliss's hands balled into fists, but Allie smiled. "He's harmless, at least to me," she said. "I'll talk to you later."

They watched the man walk away and Allie turned to glare at him again. "What are you doing here?" she hissed.

"Your mom said you're in trouble."

"She told you that?"

"Not exactly, but word gets around."

"And you're here to swoop in and rescue me." She shook her head. "You're five years too late for that, Corliss."

Now it was his turn to glare at her. "Don't pretend, Allie. You know what happened then."

"Yes, I do," she said gravely. "Which is why I want nothing to do with you now. Go home."

"Sure," he said. He allowed her to pass by him, then trailed close behind her, almost nipping her heels. She stopped short and he did, too, to avoid slamming into the back of her.

"Why are you following me?" she asked.

"I'm going home. Oh, did you forget that since we're still married and you haven't moved, my name is still on the deed to our apart-ment? How is the old home place, anyway?"

"Stop it, Corliss," she said. Her voice was tremulous, and his gut clenched. He had never been able to stand to see her cry. He also knew that she would rather die than have her hardcore, tough-as-nails prosecutor image ruined in front of her coworkers. He grabbed her hand and led her at a trot to the stairwell.

She sniffled when they paused at the top of the stairs, pressing her fingers to her eye sockets to try and stop her tears. "I can't do this; I can't handle this right now."

He took in a breath and tried to push down his anger and his hurt. He was here to help her, not to make her life more difficult. "Why don't you tell me what's been happening," he said. "Why are you in trouble?"

"I'm not sure I am. A judge was killed. He had presided over a case I was working on, and I started receiving some threats. But I always receive threats, and there's no way to know if my threats are related to his death. I wouldn't have told Mom, but sometimes they target fami-lies, and I wanted her to be on the lookout for anything unusual, in case."

"Do they target husbands?" he asked icily. "Did it ever occur to you to warn me?"

She let out a pent up breath. "You're only my husband in the most technical sense of the word. If I thought you were in any danger, then of course I would have told you."

He forced himself to relax until she spoke again.

"Look, Corliss, you have to leave. I suppose I appreciate your misguided attempt to try and protect me, but you and I have proven we can't be together without killing each other. Go home, and we'll pretend this whole thing never happened."

He stared at her, debating with himself. Clearly she wasn't in any mortal danger. On the other hand, now that he was here, he found he didn't want to leave yet. He wanted to see for himself that she was okay.

"I'm not going until I'm satisfied that everything is okay with you."

Allie wanted to stamp her foot in frustration. "Corliss, go home," she commanded, pointing at the door behind him like he was an errant puppy.

He quirked an eyebrow at her. "Let's review, Allie. Have you ever been able to get me to do what you wanted by telling me to do it?"

"No," she said, sagging dejectedly. "But what if I asked, no, begged you to leave. Please, Corliss, please go away. My life is finally in order, and I cannot have you mess it up again." Her eyes were round and soft, her hands clasped at her chest, but instead of being swayed, he was irritated.

"I'm not the one who messed up your life in the first place."

She dropped her hands with a frown. "You practically forced me to marry you when I said I wasn't ready."

"Be serious, Allie. When have I ever been able to force you to do something you didn't want to? And it wasn't our marriage that ruined our relationship."

She clammed up then, not wanting to talk about what had gone wrong between them. "Go home."

"Fine. Let's go home. Want to grab a pizza?"

Air hissed through her teeth like a pressure cooker letting off steam. Her eyes were squinched tightly closed, along with her fists. Maybe if she took him home with her for a couple of days, he would see there was really nothing the matter. He would go away, and she could try to forget him again. She shook her head. Forgetting Corliss Honeywell was like trying to forget to breathe, but at least she wouldn't have to be tortured with daily sightings if he went home.

She stalked away without answering, knowing he would follow.

"Is *Izzy's* still around?" he asked.

Izzy's had been their favorite pizza place during his brief stay in Chicago. "It's still there," she said, though she hadn't been able to eat it since he left. Too many memories.

He folded himself into her car while she drove, navigating Chicago traffic like a pro. When they reached *Izzy's* she pulled to the side of the road, idling while he went in to pick up the pizza they had ordered ahead of time. He returned with the pizza and a couple of cans of soda, smiling fondly.

"Izzy was there, and he remembered me," he said.

Allie remained mute, focusing instead on the remaining drive to her apartment. *Their apartment,* she amended. Why hadn't she moved? Stupid, stupid, stupid. Corliss cracked open one of the sodas, toying absently with the ring on the top of the can. *Don't do it, don't do it, don't do it,* she silently pled, but of course he did. She watched as he pulled off the ring and stared at it, and she knew what he was thinking as if he spoke the words out loud.

She had watched him perform the same act on the night she graduated college, only then he had slipped the makeshift ring on her finger and proposed.

"Are you crazy? We can't get married," she had said, her heart beating a million miles a minute.

"Why not? I love you, you love me. You've been my best friend for six years. Every day of those six years has been leading up to marriage. Your mom is in town. I can call my parents and have them here tomorrow. Let's do it, Allie."

She shook her head. "No, Corliss. This isn't a good time. I'm about to start law school."

"So? Who says you can't go to law school while you're married? I'll move here, we'll get an apartment. Maybe I'll go to graduate school while you're in law school. You've been pushing me to get my doctorate since we met; now's my chance."

"And what are we supposed to live on? Love?"

"I have enough in my savings to pay for our living expenses the next few years. We'll take out loans for school, then when we're done, we can go back to Kentucky. I'll return to work on the farm and you can get a job in Lexington."

"You've really covered all the bases," she said uncomfortably. Somehow, he made something crazy sound not only doable, but reasonable. Why should they wait to get married? She had loved him for six years; what difference would three years make? Right now three years seemed like forever, especially when she felt almost giddy with love.

"I'll marry you on one condition," she said.

"What?" he asked, already smiling in triumph at her quick agreement.

"I don't want to have kids until I finish school and have a couple years of work under my belt." She bit her lip, waiting for his answer. All the Honeywell men loved kids; it was a well-known fact.

"Fine," he said.

"Fine?" she echoed, incredulous.

"Allie, you're twenty-two. That's a little young for kids. And what makes you think I don't want you to follow your dreams? Being a prosecutor is as important to me as it is to you. I'm going to do anything and everything in my power to make sure you succeed, even if that means being your silent cheerleader who cooks supper on the nights you're too busy."

"You'll cook?" she asked, swept away by his tender, loving look.

"I'll cook, I'll clean, I'll rub your feet. I'll even do windows. I'll do whatever you want me to do, be whatever you want me to be. I want to be with you. Waiting for you is killing me. Please say yes."

She had to wait to blink back a couple of tears. She had glimpsed Corliss's loving and romantic side, but had never felt the full effect. Now she felt a little overwhelmed, and oh-so-in-love. "Yes," she whispered.

He was already holding her, but he gripped her tighter, lifting her feet off the ground so she was eye level with him. "You won't regret it," he returned in a whisper. "I promise, Allie. I'll love you till the day I die, and I'll make you happy." He had kissed her then, and everything else faded into oblivion.

CHAPTER 8

$\mathcal{B}$eing back in the apartment was surreal. Everything was exactly the same, yet different somehow. Allie hadn't added more furniture than the pieces they had first chosen together, but she had added other decorative touches and put her stamp on everything. There was one bedroom. Allie tried to avoid it, but Corliss poked his head in anyway. The bed was still there, and the sight pained him. They had ordered a custom-made bed, one that would fit his tall size and beyond. It had been intended to be a family bed, one where they could gather all their children on Saturday mornings. Now it belonged solely to Allie, who was so tiny she must feel lost in it at night.

She stood behind him and pointedly cleared her throat, drawing him away from the bedroom. He followed her back to the living room and deposited his bag beside the couch. His wounds once again felt raw, the edges frayed as if he had removed a bandage. Coming here was painful, but maybe it would somehow help him heal. He hoped so, because he didn't think it was possible to feel much worse. He shouldn't have opened his mouth, shouldn't have spoken, but the words leaked out before he could stop them.

"How many other men have slept in my bed since I left it, Allie?"

In response, she slapped him. Hard. Normally her small hand wouldn't have made much of an impact, but since his jaw was broken, he saw stars and everything went black for a second. He grimaced, pressing his hand over his cheek.

"Oh," Allie gasped. "Did that actually hurt you?"

"My jaw is broken," he murmured.

"Oh," she repeated again. "Sit down." He sank to the couch as she scurried to the kitchen she retrieved an ice pack, wrapped it in a dish towel, and pressed it to his cheek. He held his hand over hers to get the right amount of pressure.

"I'm sorry, Corliss," she said after a moment of silence. "I shouldn't have hit you. I've never hit anyone before, you know."

He nodded, his eyes still closed. He should apologize to her, too, but he couldn't bring himself to do it until he had an answer to the question. Did she date other men? Did she bring them here to their apartment?

As the pain in his cheek began to ebb, he became cognizant of her nearness. The smell of her perfume was different, but he liked it. She smelled like sunflowers, a scent that suited her. He opened his eyes and swallowed hard, staring into her remorse-filled eyes. She offered him a tentative smile, and he returned it.

"How did you break your jaw?" she asked.

"Brent punched me," he said.

"He punched you?" she repeated.

"I asked him to. Long story. Then I re-broke it when I got into a fight with your cousin. Apparently your family is under the delusion that our breakup was my fault."

"That's because it was your fault," she said, her tone turning acid.

"How can you say that?" he asked.

She dropped the ice pack. "You're the one who left, Corliss. You're the one who went back to Kentucky."

"After you kicked me out," he said. "You told me to go, Allie, or did you forget?"

She hadn't forgotten, but she also hadn't meant it. The fact that he didn't stay and fight for her had hurt. "Let's not do this," she said wearily. "Do you mind if I change before we eat?"

He shook his head, wincing when the action jogged his jaw. "I don't think I'm going to be able to eat anyway."

She bit her lip, looking penitent. "I'm really sorry, Corliss." Tentatively, she reached up and brushed her fingers lightly on his jaw. He froze in surprise. Before he could recover enough to reciprocate the light touch, she stood and eased off the couch, closeting herself in the bedroom.

Allie leaned against the door, gulping air. She reached behind her and undid the clasp, removing the necklace that held her wedding and engagement rings. Standing on her toes, she reached for the box at the top of her closet, tucking the rings inside so quickly she had no time to see anything else. Once her rings were safely hidden, she changed into jogging pants and a comfortable t-shirt she'd owned since college, then let down her hair, sighing in pleasure when some of the tension eased from her body.

When she returned to the living room, Corliss was sitting exactly where she left him, looking miserable. He looked up and froze. Longing flashed on his face before quickly being replaced by neutral indifference. In her absence, he had retrieved plates, glasses, and napkins. She opened the pizza box and set pizza on their plates. Corliss picked his up, tore off a tiny bite, and tried unsuccessfully to shove it in his mouth. She took a few bites before tossing her pizza back on the plate.

"I can't eat *Izzy's* in front of you like this. It's cruel."

"You eat," he said. "You look like you need the calories."

She ignored his criticism-cloaked concern. "At least let me make you a smoothie."

One lip curled in revulsion. "That sounds like some of your health food."

"Give it a try," she urged. "It's better than the nothing you're eating now."

"All right," he agreed, following her into the kitchen. She was disconcerted by his proximity as he filled up the small space. He watched with rapt attention as she blended yogurt, bananas, juice, strawberries, and honey. After pouring the concoction into a glass, she held it out for him and waited while he sniffed it cautiously. He took a sip and pulled it away with a considering smile.

"That's actually good," he said. "You could give your mother lessons on caring for an invalid."

"Mom's been giving you the cold shoulder, huh?"

"For five years," he said, smiling wider when she laughed. "It's not funny. I've been afraid to eat anything she sets before me for fear it's tainted with poison."

"It's about time she took my side for once," Allie said.

"Oh, she's fully on your side. Believe me." He sipped at the smoothie again. "Thanks for this, Allie." He tapped the now-empty glass. "I've been starving for weeks now."

"Yes, you're really wasting away to nothing, Corliss." She patted his stomach.

He took a step back, easing away from her touch. She cleared her throat uncomfortably and turned to the sink, cleaning up the smoothie dishes. Like always, his rejection stung, especially because she hadn't meant anything by the innocuous touch. Then a new, horrible thought struck her. He had accused her of seeing other men. Did he see other women?

"Are you dating anyone?" she asked as casually as she could manage.

"Allie," he said, his tone affronted. "What do you take me for? I'm married."

She turned to scowl at him. Why did he think she would date if he wouldn't? Another sign that he didn't think much of her as a person, as if she needed another reminder of his lack of faith in her.

He leaned one hip against the counter. "Speaking of dating people, what's the story with you and that guy?"

"What do you think?"

"You don't want to know what I think," he said tightly.

"Probably not." She shrugged. "He's a nice guy, and he's handling the investigation into the threats."

"No."

"What do you mean no? You can't make something not so by refusing to believe it."

"I can't work with him. Get someone else."

"Corliss, this isn't Silver Springs, Kentucky. You can't pick and choose who you want to handle a case. The police are overworked and overwhelmed as it is. I'm lucky he's able to devote as much time to it as he can; he's spending extra on it because we're friends."

Corliss's answering scowl was impressively scary. "Nonetheless, I can't work with him. I'll hire my own investigator."

Allie blew out a breath and shook her head. "You can't work outside the law here, Corliss. Trust Marlin to figure things out, if there's anything to figure out. He's a good officer."

He didn't answer, and she knew what that meant; his mind was made up, and he would be hiring his own investigator.

"I'm going to bed," she announced.

He checked his watch. "Isn't it only eight here?"

"Yes, but I've had a long, emotionally draining day."

"I can't go to bed this early," he said. "I'll wake up in the middle of the night."

"Then watch a movie. You know where they're kept."

"Is my John Wayne collection still here?"

She nodded.

"Watch with me."

"Corliss…" she began, but he interrupted.

"I know you're not really tired. You're trying to get away from me. Watching a movie is relaxing, and we won't have to talk."

"Okay," she agreed at last. How was he able to so easily break down her defenses and get her to do things? No one who knew her now would believe how pliable she was in his presence. It was maddening.

She perched on one edge of the couch, so tense she looked ready to flee while he put on the movie and turned on the television. Unbidden, the memory came of the day he purchased the television and hooked it up for them. She had sat in this very spot, mesmerized by the male gene that made him capable with all things electronic.

He finished and sat on the opposite end of the couch, placing his sock-clad feet between them as if he owned the place, which he did. She tried to keep up her rigid pose, but as the movie wore on she relaxed. Eventually, she curled into a ball and put her feet up, too, almost touching him, but not quite. As usually happened when they watched a movie together, they fell asleep. Allie woke sometime later with her feet stretched out the length of the couch, Corliss's hand resting on top of them. His legs were stretched out too, twining with hers and trapping her on the couch.

Now what? she thought. Obviously now that she was aware of their intimate position, she couldn't remain that way, to say nothing of the crick she would develop in her neck if she stayed. Then, remembering that Corliss slept like the dead, she stopped worrying about waking him as she disentangled her body from his. When she vacated the couch, he stretched to his full length, propping his knees on the end of the couch so his calves and feet could dangle over the side. She grabbed a quilt and draped it over him, resisting the almost overpowering urge to kiss his forehead as she slowly backed away.

CHAPTER 9

In the morning, Allie tried to sneak out of the house so she wouldn't wake Corliss. She should have known better. He was a heavy sleeper, but not a late one. When she exited her bedroom ready for the day, he was sitting at the kitchen table, sipping coffee and reading the paper. The sight, at once so familiar and so foreign to her, was like a fist to the gut. She had to resist the urge to turn and flee back to the safety of her bedroom. How many mornings had she padded from their room, only to see him sitting in that same position, smiling at her? And how many mornings had she gone forward, sat in his lap, and tipped her face up for a kiss? Not nearly enough.

"Morning," he said. He didn't smile, but she wasn't sure he was able to with his mouth wired shut. It was odd to see Corliss looking so grim, and she was glad there was a reasonable explanation. In her mind, he was almost always smiling. "What's on the agenda for today?"

"I don't know what you're doing, but I'm going to work," she said.

"I'm coming with you."

"Corliss, you can't."

"Sure I can. I want to see what cases you've been working on. I already called an investigator, and I need to gather some information to give to him."

For some reason, she had stupidly thought she would be able to go to work and escape him. She should have known better. Even if she was somehow able to escape his physical presence, he was always in her head. She would spend the day distracted by him anyway; what did it matter if he was actually present? "Fine, but please stay out of the way."

"You won't even know I'm there," he said. Then he stood, all six foot eight of him, wearing a pair of jeans and a gray shirt that snugged up against his muscled chest. He was and would always be the handsomest man she had ever laid eyes on, and there was no way he went anywhere unobtrusively.

To his credit, though, he tried to blend in, walking a couple of feet behind her, and not talking, merely observing. Still, he failed miserably. Everywhere they went, people stopped to stare at Corliss. His height, size, and commanding demeanor attracted so much attention it was like being with a celebrity. Allie remembered how, when she was a teenager, she had delighted in being with him, secretly wondering over the fact that, of all the girls in the world, he had chosen her. Now she simply wanted to fade into the background, to go back to her life of relative anonymity. She had learned the hard way that being with Corliss came with a price tag, and now she was unwilling to pay. She simply wanted him to go back to Kentucky so they could go on pretending the other didn't exist.

The feeling of being the center of attention grew worse as they entered her office. Here people knew there was something different. No longer could they speculate that there was something strange about Corliss's presence. Now people knew for sure that Allie wasn't usually followed by an almost seven-foot-tall bodyguard.

She sat in her cubicle, pointing to a chair for Corliss. In a predictably short amount of time, her friend, Bunny, popped her head over the adjoining cubicle, reminding Allie of a prairie dog. "Hi, Allison. Is this him? Is this your husband?" She turned her excited gaze to

Corliss and inspected what she could see of him. Corliss gave her a dashing smile and polite hello.

"I can see why you've been keeping him a secret," Bunny said. "This explains a lot."

"What does it explain?" Corliss asked. He rested his chin in his hand, fastening his intense gaze on Bunny who practically swooned in response.

"Stop being charming, Corliss," Allie snapped.

He shrugged. "I can't help it, Allie. Like the sun must shine, so must I charm your friends." He turned slightly to give Bunny a wink. Bunny giggled, actually giggled like a teenager.

"You're supposed to be on my side," Allie said, aghast. Bunny instantly sobered and ducked out of view behind her cubicle.

"When did you get so touchy?" Corliss asked. "And when did you start making people call you 'Allison?'"

"Five years ago when I stopped being a kid," she said.

"You're twenty seven. That's hardly old, Allie."

"Feels like it," she said absently, sorting through the mass of paperwork on her desk. Corliss watched her in silence for a while until he spoke again.

"Maybe I can go over some of your old cases and look for anything out of the ordinary," he suggested.

"Be my guest," she said. "There were over two hundred last year alone."

"Two hundred?" he exclaimed.

"And that's only a drop in the bucket. We're all overworked here. I work overtime I don't get paid for, and I still can't clear my docket. I haven't taken a vacation in…" She trailed off, realizing how she must sound to him. "Still, the job is very rewarding."

"I know; it's your dream come true," he said bitterly.

She let that slide, not wanting to get into it at work.

"Maybe I could look at the case you and the deceased judge were on together."

"I have that one here because I pulled it for Marlin." She held out a folder, and he snatched it from her fingers, slicing her index finger on the edge of the manila. She gasped and drew back her finger to study the small gash.

"Let me see it," Corliss demanded, holding out his hand.

She would have stuffed her hand behind her back, but he grabbed it and held it toward the light. "That's an ugly paper cut." He plucked a tissue from the box and held it on the wound. "Why do we keep hurting each other?" The way his eyes caught and held hers told her he was probably talking about more than the paper cut.

"I think it's fine. It's only a paper cut, after all," she said shakily.

"It's not fine," he replied. "This is the hand you use the most. Bunny," he called to her friend without taking his eyes off Allie. Bunny's head popped over the top of the cubicle again. "Do you have a bandage?" he asked.

Bunny ducked down and reappeared, a small bandage held in her hand. Corliss took it, thanked her, and applied it to Allie's wound all without breaking eye contact. When he was finished, he brought her finger to his lips and kissed it.

"I'm sorry," he whispered, well aware that Bunny was probably eavesdropping on the other side of the cubicle. "I'm not here to hurt you."

"Then why are you here?" Allie whispered.

"To help?" he said, making it sound like a question.

"I don't know how your being here is going to help anything," she said.

"I can try," he answered. "Let me try, Allie."

Were they talking about her finger? Or her cases? Or the unhealable breach between them? Allie didn't know. "You can try," she whispered, sliding the case folder across the desk to him. Returning her voice to a crisp, professional tone, she continued. "The investigators went over every detail of this case, but it's pretty straightforward. Everyone involved, even peripherally, had either a lack of motive or an alibi when the judge was killed."

"And how was he killed?" Corliss asked.

"Car bomb," she said, suppressing a shudder.

Corliss didn't try to hide his horrified reaction. "Maybe you should come home to Kentucky for a little while until this blows over."

She shook her head. "There's nothing for me in Kentucky."

"Was there ever, Allie? Or was it a stepping stone to get here?"

"I'm not sure it matters what I say, Corliss; you apparently have your own definition of me."

They retreated to their mutual corners in silence. She began working on her never-ending caseload, and he began reading the file from the case she had shared with the deceased judge.

"I have to make a phone call," Corliss said. He excused himself and walked away. Allie stared after him, feeling jealous for no particular reason. He had said he wasn't seeing anyone, but why else would he abruptly leave to make a call as if his tail were on fire?

"You're not in court today, are you?" he asked when he returned.

"No. Opposing counsel asked for a recess until Monday. Why?"

"I was wondering if you'll be getting out of here at a reasonable hour tonight."

"Why?" she asked again, and with more suspicion this time.

"We're going to a class tonight."

"We? A Class? What is it?"

"You'll see," he said cryptically. Her long-dormant heart actually fluttered in anticipation. Corliss's surprises were always interesting. Maybe they were going to a pottery or cooking class. The thought of what might be coming cheered her enough that she actually smiled for the rest of the day. Then they approached her car, and her smile died.

"Can I use a mirror?" Corliss asked when they stepped outside the building.

She fished in her purse and handed him her compact. Instead of checking his face like she supposed he might, he got down on his hands and knees in the parking garage, using the mirror to look under the car. Allie looked around in embarrassment, hoping and praying no one could see him.

"Corliss, what are you doing?"

"I'm checking for a bomb. Why are you whispering?"

"Because I don't want anyone to hear this crazy conversation. There is no bomb under my car."

"How do you know if you don't check?" he asked.

He had her there, but she still had no intention of checking her car every time she drove it. She wouldn't even know what to look for. He finished his inspection and handed her the mirror. "I assumed bombers used some tricky device that hooks into the engine, but apparently that's old school. Nowadays they have a method that goes off as soon as you open the door."

She shuddered, as she did anytime the bomb was mentioned. "What a horrible way to go," she commented.

He gave one curt nod before taking her keys and opening the passenger side for her. "Why are you driving?" she asked grumpily.

"Because I'm your husband."

The macho answer deserved a reply, but she had none to make. During the brief time they lived together as man and wife, she had delighted in hearing him refer to himself as her husband. But it had been so long that now the word was jarring. She didn't realize she was standing still, staring at him, until he lightly touched the small of her back, nudging her toward the car. She settled into the passenger seat and debated renewing the driving argument, then decided to let it go. Truth be told, she was relieved not to have to drive. She hated Chicago traffic.

"What's new at the farm?" she asked. For years, she had felt like an extension of his family. The last five years of ostracism had been painful.

"Haley came to stay a week."

"Haley? *The* Haley?"

"Brent's Haley," he said, smiling.

She returned his smile. "So she's Brent's Haley now, is she?"

"She is, but he doesn't know it yet. He's a little hung up about the age difference."

"How old is she now?"

"Twenty."

She whistled. "Twenty is young."

"Not so young. You were only twenty two when we got married."

And look how well that turned out, she started to say, but wisely refrained. "Where are you taking me?" she said instead. It felt like they had been driving forever.

"A shooting range," he said.

"Corliss," she exclaimed. "Are you serious?"

"I want you to know how to shoot, and I want you to be able to carry a gun."

"You already taught me to shoot," she said.

"Those were shotguns and rifles. I'm talking handguns."

"I don't want a handgun."

"Allie, be reasonable. I saw the way that man tried to attack you in the courtroom. You're getting death threats. The least you can do is take an interest in your own safety. You're also going to carry a stun gun and pepper spray, and it wouldn't hurt to take some self-defense courses."

"Corliss, stop." She pressed her palms to her temples. "You cannot come in here and dictate my life for me. I don't want to learn how to shoot, and I don't want to carry any of those things. You know me; do you really think I would be able to use any of those things on another person?"

"If your safety were threatened, then, yes, I do," he said. "At least I hope you would." What would happen to him if something happened to her? He would never forgive himself for not being present to take care of her. Now was his opportunity to make sure she could take care of herself, at least a little bit. He wanted to do all he could to make sure she understood what needed to be done.

They finished their trip out of town in moody silence. Corliss drove through a fast food restaurant, ordered a milkshake for himself, and turned to wait on her.

"I'll have a salad," she said.

He laughed because so little had changed in their eating habits. His meat and potatoes lifestyle had driven her crazy, and she was always trying to sneak vegetables near him in the hopes that he might actually eat one.

The class was long and boring, but they perked up when it was time to shoot. Despite her protests, Allie was intrigued by the thought of firing a handgun, even if she didn't want to carry one on her person. Corliss, of course, picked up the gun, shot the requisite number of times with one hand, and hit the center of his target every time, impressing his instructor.

"Kentucky born and bred," Corliss explained smugly.

When it was Allie's turn, she tried to mimic Corliss, bracing her feet and aiming with one hand.

"Stop," Corliss called. "You're too little to use one hand." He moved closer, standing behind her and wrapping his arms around hers. Even when she was properly braced and positioned he didn't let go, allowing his body to absorb the shocking impact from the recoil.

She emptied the clip into the target, and he showed her how to reload, bracing her when she fired again. She was glad she only had to squeeze the trigger because her brain had turned to mush. She knew she had missed him, but she didn't realize how much until he touched her. The experience was reminiscent of a desert flower, closed up and waiting for rain. One touch from Corliss was like that first drop of rain; now she was once again in full bloom. What would happen when he went away?

He lifted her ear protection and spoke. "Want to try it alone?"

"No." She answered automatically before she realized he was talking about the gun. Either way, she was tired of trying it alone. She had fought hard for her independence, only to realize she didn't want it after all.

Transversely, Corliss seemed utterly unaffected by her. He thanked and paid the teacher, collecting their certificates. "That was fun," he said as soon as they were in the car. "Admit it, you had fun, too, didn't you, sugar?"

Allie laughed. "No one has called me 'sugar' since I left Kentucky."

"Well, now, that's a real shame." He smiled and winked at her before starting the car.

He could be so charming when he wanted. No wonder she had fallen in love with him on sight and stayed that way ever since. If only they could go back to the way it had been, if only they could erase what had gone wrong between them. Her hands twisted nervously in her lap.

"Corliss," she began tentatively, "do you ever think it's possible for people to get over hurtful events?"

"Hmm," he replied vaguely.

What does that mean? "I mean, people have a great capacity to heal, both physically and emotionally. Don't you think?"

"Hmm." His eyes darted to the rearview mirror and narrowed.

His lack of response was making her nervous, causing her to ramble. "There are lots of instances of people who got over traumatic events, only to thrive later in life."

"Mmm, hmm." He pulled out his phone and peered at the screen before flipping it open and pushing a button. Now she was really miffed. Was there another woman? What else could draw him away from such a momentous discussion?

"Are you following me?" he asked with no preamble. "Well someone is," he continued. "No, it's too dark and too far away to see the plate. Three right turns. Double back and head for the police, got it." He closed the phone and gripped the steering wheel with both hands.

Allie turned to look behind them. "We're being followed?"

"Turn around and face forward," Corliss said calmly.

She did as he instructed, trying to remain calm. "Maybe they're not following us."

"We're about to find out," he said. He turned right, then turned right two more times.

"Is he still there?"

"Yes," he answered. "Hold on, we're heading to the nearest police station. Why don't you call and give them a head's up?"

"And say what?" she said. "That we're maybe being followed by a car we can't describe? They have too much to do to chase down those kinds of calls. Believe me; I know what they deal with on a daily basis."

His grip tightened on the steering wheel. "It's no way to live your life, Allie, when you can't count on police protection. You shouldn't be living in this city alone."

Allie crossed her arms over her chest. "I didn't start out here alone. My husband left me."

He actually flinched. "That's not what happened, and you know it."

"I know no such thing," she argued.

He took a couple of deep breaths through his nose. "Now isn't the time for this discussion."

"Is there ever a time?" she mumbled.

A few turns later, he pulled into a police station, but their tail had long ago given up pursuit. He parked the car and they sat in silence for a couple of minutes.

"I'm sorry I snapped at you," he said at last. "In answer to your first question, yes, I think it's possible to heal from terrible pain. And, yes, our time to talk about it is coming soon. But not right now. First things first, we need to figure out who's following you and why."

Slowly, he reached over and clasped her hand, bringing it to his lips for a gentle kiss. In the eleven years she had known him, it was the first time Allie had ever seen him tentative. Her heart melted a little as she realized he was as vulnerable as she was.

CHAPTER 10

$\mathcal{B}$y the time they arrived back at their apartment late that night, they were exhausted. Allie was glad it was Friday. Out of the corner of her eye, she watched as Corliss peeled off his outer clothing and tried to fold himself onto the couch.

"Take the bed, Corliss," she said. "You don't fit on the couch; you never have."

He looked up at her with a mischievous grin. "We could share the bed."

She froze. "Uh…"

"I meant that in the best possible way. That bed is huge, even for me. We could each stake out a corner and never have to touch. It could be like a campout."

Instinctively she knew it was a horrible idea, but she bit her lip, thinking about it anyway. Corliss couldn't sleep on the couch, and she really didn't want to. It wasn't a comfortable couch for sleeping. One of them could sleep on the floor, but she didn't want that either. And he was right; the bed was huge. They had wanted to make sure to get something that would accommodate his larger size, but the person who made it went a little overboard in his enthusiasm. Allie only had two sets of sheets that fit, and she'd had those custom made.

"All right," she said softly.

Corliss's triumphant smile was huge, but he quickly doused it when he saw her frown.

She changed her clothes in the bathroom, emerging in a battered nightshirt he could in no way find alluring. He lay on his half the bed and turned to face her when she joined him, pillowing his head on his hand. "This is the line," he said, drawing an imaginary line down the center of the bed. "Don't cross it."

"What happens if I cross it?" she asked with some of her old sauciness.

"Try it and find out," he taunted.

She rolled her eyes as if the idea was absurd, but it would be a lot easier to ignore the suggestion if he slept in more than his boxer shorts. "You could try wearing clothes," she said.

"I am wearing clothes," he said. "Or have you forgotten how I usually sleep?"

She reached to douse the lamp on her bedside, hiding her pink cheeks. "I haven't forgotten," she muttered.

In the darkness, she heard him chuckling softly.

She lay there so long listening to his deep, even breathing that she was sure he was asleep. Then he startled her by whispering her name.

"Allie."

"What?"

"I love this bed. I've missed it." A few seconds later, his soft snores told her he was finally asleep.

"It loves and misses you, too," she whispered, then she rolled away from him and fell asleep, too.

In the morning, Corliss woke first. He rolled toward Allie and unabashedly stared, enjoying the sight of her first thing in the morning. He had always woken first, and he always took a couple of minutes to look at her, enjoying the fact that she was beautiful and she was his. She lay on her stomach, her sleep-tousled long hair a curtain over her face. He wanted to sweep her hair aside so he could see her face, but he couldn't cross the line, either real or imaginary, and it was killing him.

Being near her but not with her was torture. There was a part of him that wanted to forget everything that had passed between them, reach out to her, and force things through until they reached an understanding—the understanding being that he was her husband and not going anywhere. But how could he forgive her for what she had done? And even if he could forgive, how could he forget? That one horrible moment hung between them, tainting all their good memories with bad. Five years hadn't worked to make it go away, although it had lessened some of the pain. He could be near her and not hate her. But he couldn't understand her. Why had she done it?

Before being married, Corliss had never believed in divorce or even separation, and certainly not from Allie, his best friend and the love of his life. But no one told him that some events are so painful they circumvent all the ethical codes one might construct.

As if sensing his thoughts about her, she opened her eyes and blinked sleepily. "Morning," she whispered, smiling slightly.

"Morning," he said, but with no answering smile. His memories had wiped all traces of grace he had previously been willing to offer. She swallowed hard and tucked her hands under her chin, almost as if she were hunching forward protectively over her heart.

"What do you want to do today?" she whispered.

"You tell me; it's your city."

Had his tone been clipped? It must have because her eyes grew large and pensive, shimmering with something that looked a lot like unshed tears. "We could go our separate ways. I always have work that needs doing. You could explore Chicago and revisit some of your favorite sights."

He rolled onto his back and squeezed his eyes tightly closed, trying to regain some emotional control. "I don't want to go our separate ways. I'll do whatever you're doing." He opened his eyes and looked at her again, forcing a smile. "Do you have eggs?"

She shook her head. "I'm not a big breakfast person."

"I'll run to the market and get some things, and then I'll cook for us."

"Okay," she said softly. She remained where she was, watching him as he got out of bed and put on his clothes. Once dressed, she thought he would simply leave, but he surprised her by crawling back into bed. He pushed on her shoulder to roll her onto her back.

"This doesn't have to be horrible. We can have a good day."

"Okay," she repeated, questioningly this time.

He smiled and it looked genuine, despite the restraints of his jaw wires. He leaned down to press a gentle kiss to her forehead, and then he was gone, leaving her wanting more. But that was the story of her life; she could never get enough Corliss Honeywell.

She waited until she was sure he was really gone, and then she stole out of bed, crept to her closet, and pulled out the box. The box hadn't started five years ago; it had started eleven years ago on the day she met Corliss, on the day she knew she had met the man she wanted to be with forever. Despite the fact that she and Corliss had few secrets, she had never told him about the box, had never told him how much she loved and adored him. He had been so much above her in status and age; she hadn't wanted anything to make her look like more of a silly school girl in his eyes. At least, that had been her excuse at first. After they were married, she kept the box a secret for a different reason.

She sat on the bed and opened the lid, staring at the contents, not touching anything. There was the corsage from her senior prom. She smiled when she remembered how much he hadn't wanted to go, and how much she had begged. *I'm a senior in college, Allie. How does that look?*

Like I scored a rich, older man, she had replied. He had laughed, and that was the end of the discussion.

There was the pop tab, the one he had first proposed with. The very next day, they went out and bought rings, but she had been a little sad to see the tab go. For a few minutes, they had been on the same level because a can of soda was something they could both afford. She loved her platinum and diamond engagement ring, but she would never get rid of the plain metal ring, the one that told her Corliss was so crazy in love with her he did something on the spur of the moment for once.

There were cards and notes. She had printed out all their electronic conversations during college, even the innocuous ones that gave no mention of what was between them. There was a little wooden whale, a memento from her trip to Maine. She had been so certain that weekend was the true beginning of her life with Corliss, but he had put her off. And he had been right. She had needed four years of college to spread her wings and mature. She would have resented him for tying her down if he had given in that weekend.

When she could avoid it no more, she moved on from the pleasant memories. With shaking fingers, she reached into the box and sifted to the bottom, pulling out a smaller box. She opened the box and lifted out the little silk christening gown, bringing it to her face so she could inhale. Her mind always played tricks on her at this point, imagining she could smell baby powder on the little garment, even though it had never been worn. She pressed the gown to her cheek, letting the memories wash over her like acid rain.

CHAPTER 11

If Allie had any lingering doubts about marriage, the first three months of newlywed bliss worked to erase them. She was as happy with Corliss as she always dreamed she would be. Since it was summer and neither was in school yet, they spent their days rapturously exploring Chicago, seeing all the sights the big city had to offer. To her amazement, Corliss seemed to be enjoying the city as much as she was. Then again, everything about Corliss amazed her.

He had declared that since his master's program was bound to be less stressful than law school, he would take over the task of cooking for them. Suspicious of his generous offer, she finally got him to admit he had always wanted to learn to cook, but had never felt comfortable taking up the hobby without a substantial reason. Less than a week after their wedding, he seemed to have mastered the kitchen and was now a budding gourmand, soaking up as much information about food and cooking as possible. The kitchen was littered with books and magazines from the library, and the television was almost always tuned to the cooking channel.

"I'm a kitchen widow," she complained on more than one occasion when he lost himself in his new hobby. He would always put down what he was doing and kiss her until she reneged her statement, then he would smugly

state that she didn't complain when she was eating his cooking. That was certainly true; he was a talented chef.

School started for her. It was as difficult and stressful as she had imagined it would be. The amount of reading alone was enough to break her, to say nothing of the classes where she felt like she was over her head. Her teachers preferred the Socratic method, calling out questions the students had better be prepared to answer, or else suffer their wrath. She felt like she was fighting not merely to keep up, but to stay one step ahead. Corliss started school, too, but he laughed off her suggestion that he was under the same amount of stress.

"I'm reading literature from before the industrial revolution," he said. "What could be stressful about that?"

She allowed herself to believe his assurances that the reason he wasn't struggling was because his school wasn't as difficult and not because she wasn't as smart as he was. Still, she had her doubts.

After the first week of school, she caught a cold that wouldn't go away. It left her feeling so rundown and exhausted she could barely manage to stay awake in class, let alone put in the long hours required to do her homework and reading.

For three weeks she struggled, vainly taking vitamins and loading up on orange juice. And then it hit her--she didn't have a cold; she was pregnant. She didn't know how she knew, she just did. Even though they had taken every possible precaution, she was married to a man who had five siblings. Fertility ran rampant in the Honeywell family, apparently. A test from the drugstore confirmed her worst fear, and Allie had a complete breakdown. She was already exhausted and under pressure. How was she supposed to add a baby into that mix?

That was how Corliss found her when he came home that night, curled up in the fetal position on the bathroom floor, crying her eyes out.

"I'm pregnant," she blurted before he could ask what was wrong. He stood in the doorway, shocked speechless for a few seconds, then he went forward and gathered her close, wiping her face with the tail of his shirt.

"It's going to be okay." He said it calmly, but she could hear the suppressed glee in his voice, and it made her furious. How could he be happy about this?

"It's not going to be okay, Corliss. I'm already drowning. How am I supposed to handle being pregnant, too? Do you know how my professors are going to look at me when I start showing? Status is important. I'm going to be the dumb kid who got herself knocked up her first year of law school. I can't do this. I can't handle this right now. Please." She pressed her face to his shirt and wept. She had no idea what she expected him to do about the situation, but she hated feeling helpless and at the mercy of something growing inside her, something she didn't want.

As ever, Corliss remained patient. For a long time, he held her and let her cry. Then when she had some semblance of control, he laid out his plan for how they would cope. *"You'll be finished with this year by the time the baby comes. You'll have the entire summer off to heal and get adjusted, and then you'll go back. I'll drop out of school and stay home with the baby."* She had tried to object, but he shook his head. *"Allie, I'm a farrier. That's all I'm ever going to be. I'm getting my master's because I'm here, and because it's fun, and not because I ever intend to do anything with it. Who cares if I drop out? You're the one with the career ambition. It's not going to be easy, but we'll manage. After you finish law school, we'll move back to Kentucky, and we'll have all sorts of help on the farm. We have to put our heads down and make it for three years, and then we're in the clear."*

"But what if I get pregnant again after this one?" she had said, panicked. *"What if I'm one of those women who has a baby every year?"*

He was quiet for a second, and when he spoke, she realized she had offended him. *"Like my mom?"*

She swallowed hard. How could she explain to him that it wasn't his mom she didn't want to end up like; it was her mom. All her life, she had watched her mother struggle to provide, to make it as a single mother. Allie had never even known her father, had never seen him, never talked to him. She had vowed never to end up like her mom who had dropped out of high school to have Allie when she was only seventeen. No, that life wasn't for Allie. She wasn't the stupid girl who got pregnant and ruined her future; she was driven and ambitious. She would succeed or die trying.

"That wasn't what I meant," she said, but Corliss didn't relax his rigid grip on her. She took a deep breath and tried to get a handle on her wild emotions. *"Each of us has to choose the path that's best for us, Corliss. Your*

mom made the decision to be a mother and have a lot of kids. But that's never been what I wanted, and you know that."

"I knew you didn't want as many kids as my mom had, but I thought you wanted some," he said tightly.

"I do. Just not now."

"But it's too late now, Allie. You might as well get on board because you have no choice in the matter."

"I always have a choice in the matter," she said. She had meant the words flippantly, as a last show of independence. She hadn't realized how they would sound to Corliss who abruptly stood and left the room. She sat on the floor, crying once again and staring after him, wishing she could explain her wild mix of emotions. She was shocked and upset, but it didn't mean she wouldn't eventually get over it and get with the program. He was right; what choice did she have really? Why couldn't he understand this was a difficult adjustment for her? Why couldn't he give her a little time to make the adjustment? Why couldn't he be more understanding?

For two days, he remained silent and standoffish. Then when he woke in the night to find her weeping, he pulled her close and kissed her, healing over any breach that had been between them. He once again comforted her, listening to her as she poured out her worries and frustrations. She wanted to tell him that talking about it was her way of coping, that she would eventually come around and be excited about their baby, but before she could get the words out, she fell asleep.

CHAPTER 12

By the time Corliss returned, Allie's box was once again well hidden on the shelf.

"I picked up your mail," he said, slapping it on the kitchen table as he passed.

"You have to have a key for the mailbox," she said, mystified.

"I still had my key. I remembered when I passed. It's nice to know what one of the keys on my ring is for. There are so many now, I've lost track." As he spoke, he deftly cracked eggs in a bowl, stirring them with a whisk. She sat at the table and propped her head in her hands, watching.

"Do you ever cook at home?"

"No. To this day, no one has any idea I can cook. It's our little secret." He gave her a wink over his shoulder. She smiled half-heartedly. They had too many secrets that were their own, as far as she was concerned. At least, she hoped they were still their secrets.

"Why did you tell your parents you went home?" she asked.

"I told them things didn't work out. They didn't ask questions." She sagged in relief until he continued. "I told my brothers the truth, though. We don't keep secrets."

Her brow puckered in concern. The truth from his point of view wasn't exactly the truth. She loved his brothers as if they were her own. She didn't want them to think badly of her.

"What was their response?" she asked.

"Sympathy. For both of us. They said you must have been under a whole lot of stress." He paused, flipping the omelet in the pan. "I guess you were under more stress than I even realized. I'm sorry about that."

"Please don't," she choked. "Don't apologize, Corliss. You were supportive and wonderful during that time. No one could have been a better husband."

"Then why…" He wrenched the words out, cutting them off before he could finish. "Never mind," he said with forced calm. He plated their omelets, setting the stuffed one before her and taking the plain one for himself. She thought at first he had made a mistake because he liked his eggs loaded, but then she realized he probably couldn't chew anything besides the fluffy egg. She covered his hand with hers and gave it a squeeze.

"Thank you. I'm sorry about your jaw. How much longer do you have to keep the wires on?"

"Two more weeks," he said. He returned the pressure on her hand and held onto it, eating with his left hand. Even though they didn't talk while they ate, the company was nice, as was the touching. Allie had been so lonely the last few years without him. It was as if she had been in solitary confinement, unable to go home to Kentucky for fear of seeing him or his family, unable and unwilling to date. If not for her friends, she would probably only talk to street thugs and cops at her job.

Allie finished eating long before poor Corliss who had to cut his food into tiny bites and shove it between the cracks in his wires. She picked up her mail and began to sort it, her hand suspending in midair when she reached a familiar-looking envelope.

Ever perceptive to her moods, Corliss noticed. "What is it?"

"It looks like some of the other threats I've received," she said, carefully setting it aside.

"Aren't you going to open it?"

She shook her head. "Marlin asked me to bring all correspondence to him so I don't corrupt it with fingerprints. I should call and see if he's in today."

"On a Saturday?"

"He works odd hours. He's very dedicated."

"He sounds like a saint," Corliss said bitterly.

She found his jealousy irritating. "You have no right to waltz in here after five years and try to pretend you care what's going on in my life."

"You know I care. And if you didn't want me to, you would have divorced me long ago."

They squared off over the table, frowning at each other and breathing hard. Her phone rang and she lunged for it, picking it up before it finished one ring. "Hello."

"Allison, it's Marlin."

Her face relaxed into a smile. "I was going to call you."

Corliss stood and began loudly clearing the dishes.

"Is now a bad time to talk?" Marlin asked.

"No." She rose and moved into the living room. "In fact, it's sort of necessary. I received another letter this morning."

"You did?" he asked, tense. "Can you bring it into the station?"

"Yes, I can, and I should also tell you that we were followed last night."

"We?"

"My…husband and I."

There was a significant pause. "So you really are married to that guy."

"Technically speaking, yes."

There was another pause before he spoke again. "I guess I sort of thought you and I were headed somewhere."

"I'm sorry if I gave you that impression, Marlin. You've been a very good friend to me, and if, well…Things are complicated between Corliss and me, but I'm still very much attached. I won't date while I'm still married, even if we are separated." She realized she was rambling nervously and tried to put a cap on it.

"Oh," Marlin answered, clearly disappointed and possibly a little angry. "I'll see you this afternoon." He hung up without saying good-bye. She closed the phone, feeling guilty. Had she somehow led Marlin on? She thought she had kept things strictly professional, but in retrospect they had worked a few late cases together, and they had eaten supper while they worked. But he didn't count those as dates, did he? She hadn't flirted, and they had never touched.

"Ready?" Corliss asked. His crisp tone told her that he was also angry with her.

"Ready," she replied. Why did this have to happen now? Why this week of all weeks? Had Corliss planned it to coincide with tomorrow? She had already planned to spend the day in her apartment, moping. Did he show up in order to heap misery on her already miserable head? Guilt on her already guilty conscience?

The drive to the police department was tense and silent, and Corliss's mood didn't improve once they arrived. He looked menacing as he broodingly hovered behind Allie, his arms crossed over his chest. Today she didn't think his grim look was from his jaw being wired shut.

She led the way to Marlin's desk. Marlin looked up to greet them with a similarly dissatisfied expression that grew worse when Corliss held Allie's chair for her. To her relief, after he sat down, Corliss seemed content to stay quiet and observe, or so she thought.

"Here it is," Allie said nervously as she handed over the newest letter she had received.

"Thank you," Marlin said, setting it aside.

Corliss shifted in his chair. "Aren't you going to open it?"

"I'll open it later," Marlin said.

"I would prefer that you open it now," Corliss said.

"I don't work for you," Marlin replied evenly. Allie knew him well enough to know he was keeping a barely controlled leash on his temper.

"All the same, I would like to see what's in the letter. If I had known you weren't going to open it for us, I would have opened it myself," Corliss said.

"And that would have contaminated any trace of fingerprints," Marlin said.

"Do you actually plan to dust it for prints? From what Allie has told me, y'all are overworked as it is."

Allie turned back to Marlin with a considering frown. *Was* he dusting the letters for prints?

"I dusted the first few for prints," Marlin replied testily.

"And what did you find?" Corliss asked.

"There were no prints," Marlin ground out.

"If there were no prints, then why can't Allie open the letters for herself?" Corliss pressed.

Marlin took a breath, held it, and released it slowly. "Listen, Mr. Honeywell, why don't you let me do my job and stop trying to complicate it with your testosterone?"

Corliss blinked at him, a sure sign *he* was keeping a short leash on his temper. "Testosterone has nothing to do with wanting to keep my wife safe," he said quietly.

Marlin leaned back, templing his fingers and regarding Corliss with a speculative glare. "It's strange, Mr. Honeywell, that you've come back when Allison started receiving these threats."

Corliss didn't reply. He merely held Marlin's unblinking stare.

"I did some checking on you; you've been arrested quite a number of times for brawling."

"You would be hard-pressed to find any charges that have stuck," Corliss replied mildly.

"Money talks, even in Kentucky, I'm sure. The point is that, from a detective's point of view, you can see how suspicious it looks for a missing spouse, one who has a history of violence, to return at such a precipitous time."

Allie wanted to say something, to defend Corliss, but Corliss had never needed her defense, which he proved when he smiled slightly and spoke.

"As we say in Kentucky, sir, you're barking up the wrong tree. I've hired an outside investigator, and I do hope you'll give him your full cooperation."

That was when Marlin's control snapped. His face turned puce. He leaned forward so hard that the front two legs of his chair slammed against the ground. "You had no right..." he began, jabbing a finger at Corliss.

"I have every right where my wife's safety is concerned. Allie tells me you're good at your job, and I don't doubt her judgment. But she's also told me you're overworked with barely enough time to look into her case. I want someone who will devote his full efforts to clearing up this matter. And I also want someone who isn't in love with my wife."

"Corliss," Allie said, but he ignored her and stood, holding out his hand to her. She put her hand in his and stood, figuring it was best for everyone if they left as soon as possible.

"One more thing, sir," Corliss added before they left. "I would leave the cross examinations to my wife; she's much better at it." With that, he tucked Allie's hand in his elbow and led her from the building.

"That was unnecessary and rude," Allie said as soon as she was safely tucked in her car—the *passenger* seat of her car.

"That was completely necessary and far from rude," Corliss contradicted. "Besides, he started it."

"Corliss, you cannot go around Chicago like a rutting bull, challenging every man I may have talked to in the last five years."

"How many men have there been?" he asked, renewing the question she had never answered.

She looked out the window and scowled, vowing herself to silence. The car screeched to a halt before whipping into a parking place. Corliss slammed from the car, opened her door, unfastened her seatbelt and pulled her outside. He towered over her, pressing her against the side of the car.

"How many, Allie? We're not moving until you tell me."

She glared at him, wishing she were as strong as he was. He wasn't hurting her, but it wasn't his physical strength she resented; Corliss had always been the one with more inner power and resolve. He had held out for six years, not kissing her even when she begged. She wanted to hold out now, to remain stoic on the topic of who she had dated, but as she looked in his coal-black eyes, she saw that they were tinged with pain, and her resolve broke.

"No one," she said softly. "There's been no one, Corliss. How could you think so little of me?" Traitorous tears shimmered in her eyes.

He closed his eyes, sagging in relief so that even more of his weight was pressing on her. Her hands slipped between them to try and push him away, but once they settled on his chest, she lost the will to try. He was so solid, warm, and vital. His large size encompassed her. By all rights she should feel constricted by the weight of his solid mass, but she didn't. She felt safe, cared for, and protected for the first time in a long, long time. Before she could talk herself out of it, she closed her eyes and rested her forehead on his chest, inhaling his pleasant scent. He didn't wear cologne; he simply smelled like Corliss.

He bowed his head and rested it beside hers, his lips close to her ear. "I'm sorry," he murmured. "I'm not exactly rational when it comes to you." His hands slipped to her waist and gave her a squeeze. "Thank you for telling me."

"You left me no choice," she said.

"You always have a choice," he replied, and they both stiffened. Whether or not he had intentionally brought up the words she had used when they found out about the baby, she didn't know. She didn't think so, but it worked as a reminder all the same. To her shame, she clung to him, clutching his shirt in her fists, but it did no good. He eased away from her and opened her car door. Like that, the reprieve was over and they were back to being impolite strangers.

Allie stared out the window in sullen silence, and Corliss did nothing to try and pull her out of her mood. She felt like she was spiraling out of control. Tomorrow was already going to be difficult, and now she had Corliss here to make the memories more potent. She wanted nothing more than to closet herself in her room and weep-- weep for herself, for Corliss, for all they had lost, and for all that had gone wrong between them. Corliss, however, had other ideas.

The car stopped and Allie looked around in confusion. "What are we doing?" she asked.

"We're going to play basketball," he said.

She quirked an eyebrow as she looked him up and down, taking in his height. "You know you're fourteen inches taller than me, right?"

He smiled. "We're about to level the playing field, sugar."

She stayed put while he came around to her side and opened her door with a smile. "You're starting to remember," he said, and then laughed when she rolled her eyes. The first few months of their friendship, he had taught her that she was to stay seated in the car until he came to retrieve her. When she had argued that the practice was archaic, he had replied that the practice was southern and she was living in the south.

She chuckled, remembering something else. "My freshman year of college, I went on a date and stayed in the car, waiting for the guy to come get me. He tapped on my window and asked me if I was sick and that was why I wasn't getting out." They laughed together and she shook her head, frustration mixing with her amusement. "Your rules never carried over into anyone else, you know."

He slipped his arm around her shoulders and gave her a squeeze. "Is that your way of telling me I'm one of a kind?"

She didn't answer, not wanting to puff up his head any more than it already was. But the answer was yes, Corliss Honeywell was definitely one of a kind. Even with four brothers who looked and acted almost exactly the same, there was no mistaking any of them for Corliss. And she should know; she had grown up with them as much as him. "Tell me more about Haley and Brent," she begged, suddenly homesick and desperate for any news about home.

He launched into a long narrative about Haley and Brent, ending with the fact that Haley was currently giving Brent the cold shoulder and ignoring his calls.

Allie whistled appreciatively. "Ignoring a Honeywell when he beckons is not for the faint-hearted. I think I like this Haley girl."

Corliss smiled, ignoring her insult. "I think you would like her. She's a sweet girl, and she's mellow."

Allie nodded. Being mellow would go a long way for whomever a Honeywell married. She sighed. "I'm not mellow," she muttered.

He gave her shoulders another squeeze. "I like you mighty fine, Mrs. Honeywell."

There, it happened again, that burst of adrenaline that hearing her married name had caused during the brief time they lived together. To her chagrin, she felt herself blushing like a schoolgirl and looked away, trying to hide it. That's when she realized where they were.

"Trampoline basketball?" she asked, not at all sure how she felt about it.

Corliss nodded. "Trampoline basketball," he repeated happily. "Trust me; you're going to love it."

She relaxed because usually if he said she was going to love something she ended up doing so, and today was no exception. She and Corliss played one on one on a large round trampoline with baskets on either side. His height still gave him a slight advantage, but not as much as on a regular court. Her smaller size gave her more dexterity and she was able to flit around him, making baskets behind his back while he tried to turn himself mid-bounce. After a couple of games—which he won by a surprisingly low margin—they lay on the trampoline, too exhausted to do more than laugh. The game had been exhilarating and what she needed to work out much of her anxiety.

"Thanks for this, Corliss. It was fun."

He snagged her hand, twining their fingers together. "You're welcome." He squeezed her hand and she rested her head on his shoulder, smiling.

"What now?" she asked, and she wasn't sure she was talking about their immediate future. What happened after this pleasant interlude? Did he return back to Kentucky as if they were still enemies? Did he stay here and try to make a go of it? After the pleasant morning that had released so many endorphins, she felt ready to tackle their issues, but apparently Corliss didn't.

"Now we eat," he said. "I'm starving."

"Let's get smoothies," she suggested. "I know a good place."

"I don't know," he drawled.

She rolled toward him, propping her elbows on his chest. "Corliss, I can't stand to see you picking at your food and trying to stuff bird bites into your mouth. Can you trust me for once and get a protein-filled smoothie? It will taste good, I promise."

He smiled at her, framing her face with his hands. She froze, her heartbeat accelerating to stroke level. He kissed his fingertips and pressed them to her lips. "My jaw is broken," he reminded her. She bit her lip and studied him, smoothing her finger over his bottom lip. Maybe it was for the best that he couldn't kiss her. Who knew where it might lead? Well, she knew exactly where it would lead, and she definitely didn't think they were ready for that.

He traced his finger gently over her features. "You get prettier every year, Allie," he said softly.

She smiled. "My jaw's not broken," she reminded him, then she leaned up and pressed her lips to his. He gripped her biceps, becoming noticeably still beneath her. Allie realized then that his jaw excuse had been that—an excuse. The fact that he was unable or unwilling to kiss her had nothing to do with a broken bone. She moved away from him, attempting to ignore his silent rebuff.

"Allie," he began, but she glibly talked over him.

"Let's go; I'm hungry," she lied. While a few minutes ago she had been ravenous, she now didn't think she would be able to eat a bite. She hopped off the edge of the trampoline and practically sprinted to the exit, Corliss plodding slowly behind.

CHAPTER 13

*L*unch was a quiet, tense affair. Corliss tried to cajole Allie from her dark mood.

"Which smoothie do you recommend?"

Her lip twitched in a slightly upward motion at the way he said "smoothie," as if it were a disease. She was tempted to recommend something with tofu and wheat grass, but took pity on him. He had to be starving. Instead she recommended something with fruit, yogurt, and protein powder that was sure to put a dent in his lingering hunger.

For herself, she ordered the wheat grass and tofu concoction, and found a table while Corliss waited for their order. He held hers out in front of him as if it were contagious as he approached the table.

"That's an unhealthy shade of green," he commented as he set the drink down before her.

"Want to taste?' she asked tauntingly.

His lip curled in disgust, as much as it could. "Did you know they actually put grass in that? I could feed it to the horses. Have you become a vegetarian?"

She hadn't, but she was in a raging bad mood and spoiling for a fight. "So what if I have?"

"That doesn't seem healthy," he said mildly, eyeing her cautiously as he sipped his smoothie.

She sighed, suddenly lacking the energy to spar with him. Instead, she glanced out the window, deflated.

"C'mon, Allie, what happened to your spunk? Where's your fighting spirit?"

"I save it for the courtroom now," she said listlessly. Outside she saw a mother pushing a stroller and the vision brought stinging tears to her eyes. Corliss followed the line of her gaze with a pain-filled grimace of his own. They finished their smoothies in heavy silence.

Allie felt the need to flee. She had no idea where she could go, only that she was desperate to get away from Corliss. And since he was the one who was causing the problem, he should be the one to leave.

"Allie," he started when they stepped outside the smoothie shop. His serious tone told her she didn't want to hear what came next, no matter what it was.

"You have to go," she blurted.

He stopped short and looked down at her. "What?"

"You heard me. You have to go. Nothing is happening here. Marlin has the case under control. Your presence is redundant."

His frown deepened to a scowl. "But I thought we…"

"What?" she interrupted again, her fire gaining fuel. "You thought we were working on us? You thought we were working things out? That ship has sailed, Corliss."

He looked thunderously angry. "Then why haven't you divorced me, Allie? If it was really over, why haven't you let me go?"

She licked her suddenly dry lips, casting about for a distraction, or answer, or anything. "Well," she began, and then she was soaring through the air, Corliss on top of her. They landed hard on the pavement with a heavy thud. His body absorbed most of the impact, but the wind was still knocked from her, rendering her speechless. When she landed, her purse went flying, its contents scattering on the pavement. In one fluid movement, Corliss dove for her phone and rolled them toward the curb, snugging them tight against the side of a car.

She watched, dazed, as he opened the phone and pushed buttons.

"Someone shot at my wife," he said.

Allie jumped, startled. Was he making that up? There had been a cracking sound, but it hadn't seemed loud to her. In fact, in the midst of her emotional meltdown, it had hardly been discernable.

"Yes, I'm injured, but not badly," he said, causing her eyes to frantically sweep over him. "Are you hurt, Allie?" he asked urgently. But she still couldn't answer. She felt as if words had no meaning for her. Anything she tried to say at this point would be gibberish.

"I don't think she's hurt," Corliss said carefully, his eyes scrutinizing her face. "I think she's in shock."

Shock? Her? How could she be in shock? She was a hardened prosecutor, known for handling the most difficult, traumatizing cases without batting an eyelash. Certainly she, Allison Miller Honeywell, wasn't in shock. She opened her mouth to say as much, and that's when she saw the blood. It pooled on Corliss's shoulder until it collected a sufficient amount, and then it dripped onto her, smacking her forehead before running down her cheek. Then the sound that came from her open mouth was an ear-splitting scream.

Corliss's hand covered her mouth. "Shhh. We don't want him to know where we are in case he's still out there."

She nodded dumbly in agreement, but she wasn't certain she wouldn't scream again when he removed his hand. "Corliss, you've been shot," she whispered hoarsely.

"Nah, the bullet glanced my shoulder. It's only a flesh wound."

If he was trying to make her laugh by quoting *Monte Python*, he failed miserably.

"Let me see," she commanded, some semblance of reason returning to her panicked brain. He arched his eyebrows in amused surprise when she ripped his shirt open to stare at the wound. There was a lot of blood, but no hole. Instead, there was one long strip, blackened on the edges as if the bullet had danced across his skin, burning him with the heat of its sizzling intensity. She gulped furiously, trying not to think of what might have been.

The sound of a siren pierced the air. An ambulance arrived, but no paramedics descended the vehicle.

"What are they waiting for?" Corliss asked irritably.

"An officer to secure the scene," she answered off-handedly. "Too many medics and firefighters have lost their lives running to a live scene while there's still danger. Don't worry; response times are good in this neighborhood."

He frowned at her, probably puzzled by her now-calm demeanor. For her part, Allie was glad to be back on familiar territory. Crime scenes were nothing new to her. From here on out, she knew what to expect.

A few minutes later, two uniformed cops arrived, securing their weapons as they approached Corliss and Allie. "We've swept the area. All signs of a shooter are gone now," one of them said.

Corliss pried his hands off Allie. Until then she hadn't realized how tightly he'd been holding her, or how completely his body shielded hers.

"Are you okay?" he asked as he got to his feet and put a hand down for her.

"Corliss, you've been shot. A little less machismo, please."

He smiled wryly. "It doesn't hurt a wink. I don't even need a bandage."

"Sir, I really think you should have that looked at," one of the officers said, staring in concern at Corliss's blood-soaked shirt.

"He was kidding," Allie said. "Of course he's going to have it looked at." And, knowing Corliss, he was probably also in a lot of pain but would never say a word about it.

She walked with him to the waiting ambulance. The EMT's emerged, looking impatient. Allie knew it was hard on them to remain inactive on the sidelines when injured people needed help.

"Ma'am, are you injured?" One of them spoke solicitously to her and offered her a seat on a gurney.

She took the seat but shook her head. "I'm fine, really. Please see to my husband."

"It only takes one of them to tend to my wound, Allie. Let the man examine you," Corliss commanded.

Allie clamped her lips together but allowed the amused EMT to look her over. "You sound like me and my wife," he said, chuckling.

"How long have you been married?" she asked.

"Ten years," he replied. "You?"

"Five," she replied.

"Any kids?" he asked.

She shook her head, not trusting herself to speak.

"You're wise to wait," the man said. "I love my brood, but having kids certainly changes things."

Allie couldn't help it; she glanced at Corliss. He was looking at her, his expression dark and intense. She looked away, shuddering, and the medic thankfully changed the subject.

"You have a goose egg on the back of your head, but otherwise I think you're fine. Of course, the doctor will have the final say on that."

Allie shook her head. The action brought a dull ache, but nothing seriously painful. "I'm not going to the hospital, but thank you for your concern."

"Allie," Corliss said, but she held up a hand, cutting him off.

"Are you going?" she asked.

"For a cut?" he asked, incredulous.

"Well then there you go. I can be as stubborn as you."

"That's for certain," he muttered, causing the medic to chuckle again.

"Allison."

They all turned to look as Marlin arrived on the scene, sounding frantic as his eyes searched the small crowd until he found her. He jogged over, his eyes skimming her from head to toe.

"Are you all right? Are you injured?"

She shook her head and pointed toward Corliss. "Corliss was hit."

Marlin darted him a flickering glance before returning his eyes to Allie. "He looks fine."

She wanted to argue, to assert that Corliss was far from fine, but that would do nothing to help the situation.

"Did you see or hear anything?" Marlin asked.

"No," she said regretfully. Bad witnesses were the bane of her existence, and now she was one.

Marlin's answering smile was amused and she wondered if he guessed her thoughts.

"Aren't you going to ask me what I saw and heard?" Corliss asked. His accentuated southern drawl was a clear indicator that he was trying to keep his cool.

"The uniformed officers will take a formal statement. But, sure, what did you see or hear?" Marlin asked.

"I saw my life flash before my eyes, and Allie was in every moment," Corliss said, looking at her instead of Marlin. "And I heard a crack."

"You heard a crack and you automatically assumed it was gunfire," Marlin said, his tone dubious.

Corliss's eyes slid to Marlin and narrowed. "I heard a crack and *knew* it was gunfire."

"And how did you know that?"

"If you grew up in the woods of Kentucky with four brothers and a father who like to hunt, then you wouldn't have to ask. I know what gunfire sounds like."

Marlin apparently had no argument with that because he turned back to Allie with a stiff smile. "I'm glad you're okay. This is out of my jurisdiction, but I'm going to talk to the officers. Call if you need anything." He reached for her hand, thought better of it, and walked away.

The medics, who had been watching the little scene like it was a soap opera, finished their ministrations in silence. Corliss stood and lifted Allie down, giving her a squeeze with his good arm. He took her hand and held it as they gave their statements to the officers. By the time they finished, it was suppertime and they were hungry. Corliss ordered another smoothie, though he insisted Allie eat something more substantial. After picking up a fast food sandwich and salad for her, they headed home.

Without asking if it was what she wanted, Corliss put in another John Wayne movie and they settled on the couch to eat. There was silence between them, but unlike before the quiet was comfortable. They were both feeling exhausted and drained by their ordeal, and it wasn't long before their eyes started to droop.

"Want to go to bed before we fall asleep out here?" Corliss asked.

Allie nodded, too weary to speak. They headed toward the bedroom and wordlessly shared the bathroom, brushing their teeth and washing their faces. Allie saw Corliss wince when he bumped his shoulder on the doorframe and she shook some aspirin into his palm. He tossed them down his throat and sipped from the faucet, then they stumbled toward the bedroom. Corliss stripped to his boxers and Allie changed into her gown, not realizing she had done so until she saw Corliss's open-mouthed surprise. Belatedly she turned her back to him and finished dressing, cursing herself for being so comfortable with him that she had slipped into their ancient nighttime routine.

If she was under any delusion that the sight of her without clothes had tempted him beyond reason, his soft snores soon proved otherwise. She lay a couple of feet away from him, staring at the ceiling, trembling all over, trying not to make a sound.

Corliss had come so close to being killed today. What would she do without him? True, he had been absent from her life the past few years, but she knew where he was. She knew he was safe. If he was truly absent from the earth, how would she survive?

Her thoughts turned from Corliss to the miserable day that lay ahead tomorrow. How would she survive that, either? Would Corliss know? Would he remember? She was afraid he wouldn't and terrified he would. The occasion would no doubt reopen all the old wounds between them, wounds that were barely beginning to heal.

In trying so hard not to cry, she whimpered and then froze, barely daring to breathe lest she wake Corliss. She didn't want to have to talk to him right now or explain why she was so upset. Not that he would need much explanation; the day had been an ordeal.

When he reached for her, her heart jumped into her throat. He wrapped his arms around her and dragged her the distance between them, throwing his leg over both hers. She held perfectly still, squeezing her eyes shut until she realized he was still snoring softly, and then she smiled. Apparently his sleep instinct was to offer comfort, and she decided to take it in any form she could get. She chuckled softly when he gave a reassuring pat to her backside, then she turned toward him, snuggling into the niche she had discovered shortly after they were married, the one that fit her so perfectly it was as if it had been carved from his body to make room for hers. Finally safe and warm, she fell asleep, holding the terrible memories at bay until the daylight hours.

CHAPTER 14

The cramping started while Allie was still in class. At first she was so distracted by trying to follow what the professor was saying, she simply thought she was starting her period. Then, sometime later, it hit her that she wasn't supposed to start her period; she was pregnant.

As soon as class was finished, she darted out of the door and sat on a bench, floundering. What should she do? Who should she call? Corliss had been nagging her for the last few weeks to go the doctor and confirm the pregnancy, but Allie hadn't had the time. And, if she were being honest, she would also admit she hadn't had the inclination. Going to the doctor would only confirm the inevitable. It was far easier to live in her own little fantasy world, the one where everything would keep going on exactly as she had planned. But now, faced with this unknown pain, she felt panicked. Not only did she not have a gynecologist, but she didn't have a family doctor. Why should she? She was a healthy post-grad with horrible insurance.

Should she go to the emergency room? She wasn't sure, but their insurance was so bad that emergency room visits mostly came out of pocket. She would only go there as a last possible resort. As her panic started to ebb, reason began to return. The school employed a nurse; she would call the on-campus health clinic and ask them what to do.

Nervously, she tapped her foot as she waited for the nurse to answer.

When she did, Allie blurted out her story in a confusing string, not allowing for any pauses. For that reason, she had to repeat and revise the information a few times before the nurse understood it.

"How far along are you?" the nurse asked.

"I don't know," Allie said. "I haven't been to the doctor yet. But I think I'm somewhere in my first trimester." She bit her lip. Why oh why hadn't she listened to Corliss and gone to the doctor? He was going to be livid with her over this.

"Is there any blood?"

Allie swallowed hard as the nurse's urgent tone notched her panic up again. "No, there's no blood. Only a sharp twinge of pain."

"That's good," the nurse reassured her. "It could be the placenta attaching to your uterus, or it could be the tendons in the area stretching, or it could be something worse. You won't know until you see the doctor. Do you have a doctor?"

"No," Allie said, sounding as desperate as she felt. "I have no idea where to go or who to see."

"There's a doctor who sees a lot of our students. I'll give you his number and I would guess they'll try to get you in today if you're having this pain," the nurse said.

Her motherly and reassuring tone began to work its magic on Allie, and she sat back, relaxing. "Thank you," she said sincerely. She wrote down the number for the doctor and called him as soon as she hung up with the nurse. As predicted, they were able to see her that afternoon. Allie bit her lip and checked her watch. She would have to leave class early to make it on time, but now that she had made the decision to see the doctor, she decided to get it over with.

"All right," she agreed. Hanging up her phone, she scurried to her next class, trying hard to ignore the dull ache in her abdomen.

The doctor's nurse had told her to keep her feet up and relax, so that's what she tried to do while she sat in class. Her mind was distracted as her thoughts about the baby ran rampant. For the last few weeks, she had been upset about being pregnant. Things had been tense between her and Corliss, more tense than at any time in their past. He was angry with her for her denial and less-than-thrilled attitude about their child, and she was angry with him for his glee-filled excitement. But now, faced with the possibility of losing the little human inside her, she found that she desperately wanted to keep him. In a few short months, she would have a little Corliss to love and hold. The baby would no doubt be huge and she would curse Corliss and his gigantic size during the delivery, but after that she would have a dark-haired baby to cuddle, someone with Corliss's sweet and sunny temperament, someone to present to their parents as proof of their love and happiness.

She pressed her hand over her abdomen, smiling faintly. Please be okay, *she pled, not sure if she was praying or not. All she knew was that right now she wanted this baby more than anything else in the world.*

A quick check of her watch showed it to be time for her to leave. She stood as unobtrusively as possible and slipped out. She slid behind the wheel of her car, and that's when she felt it—the warm wetness seeping between her legs. The tears came unbidden, though she tried to keep them under control so she could drive. By the time she arrived at the doctor's office, she was a weeping mess. They immediately ushered her to an exam room, most likely to keep her from upsetting the other patients because she still had to wait what seemed like forever for the doctor to enter.

He performed a grim and silent physical exam before turning on the ultrasound machine and running it over her abdomen. At last he wiped off her stomach and returned the wand to its holster.

"I'm sorry to tell you, Allie, that your baby is gone. And, worse still, there seem to be parts of the placenta still lodged in your uterus. We can perform a D&C to remove these pieces now, or you can wait a few days to see if they come out on their own."

"Do it now," Allie said numbly. She didn't want to wait, knowing there was something already dead inside her, waiting for the chance to come out, and she didn't think her insurance would cover two visits.

"All right," he said. He was a kindly man, but she was beyond feeling any comfort. "You won't be able to drive home. Do you want to call your husband, or do you want my secretary to do it for you?"

"Your secretary," Allie replied, sounding as weak and afraid as she felt. How was she ever going to face Corliss? The weight of guilt pressed heavily on her head. If only she had gotten the prenatal care he had been pushing her

to find. If only she hadn't pushed herself so hard at school, if she had slept more, eaten better...something.

The doctor, as if sensing her thoughts, laid a gentle hand on her forearm. "There is nothing you could have done to prevent this, Allie. These things happen more frequently than anyone realizes. And it doesn't mean you can't try again. Lots of women who have miscarriages go on to have multiple successful pregnancies."

She nodded, trying to take heart in his words, though they did nothing to ease her stifling guilt. The procedure was only mildly uncomfortable and didn't take long. The doctor gave her a prescription for preventative antibiotics, as well as for some painkillers. She listened halfheartedly to his postprocedural instructions and gave him a vague smile when he walked her to the waiting area.

Corliss was there when she stepped out. One look at his face, and she knew he blamed her for what happened. He came forward to help her, grasping her elbow for support, but he didn't say a word. His expression was blank, which was always a bad sign. Allie felt so desperate for comfort that she almost wanted to throw herself at his feet and beg for it, but she couldn't. She had lost that right when she'd lost their baby.

He drove to the pharmacy in silence, told her to wait in the car, and went to fill her prescriptions. She rested her head on the window, closing her eyes and sending up vague prayers for help or support. She wasn't sure how she felt about God right now. She didn't feel angry; she felt chastised. Had He heard her complaints about the baby and decided to give her what she said she wanted? Had He taken her baby because she had been ungrateful for the blessing?

Or did He know her heart? Did He understand that she had simply needed some time to adjust, that once she became used to the idea, she would have loved her baby with a mother's heart—full of selfless care, the way her mother had loved her? The way Corliss's mother had loved him. Now she would never know, and the weight of having both Corliss and possibly God angry at her felt like too much.

Corliss returned to the car and set her prescriptions in her lap. "Are you hungry?" he asked.

She shook her head. The physical pain was setting in. The doctor had told her there might be cramping, but she hadn't realized it would be so bad. She unscrewed the pain reliever and downed two dry. Each spasm in her belly sent an echoing spasm to her heart, reminding her of the emptiness in both. She had lost her baby, and she had lost Corliss. She didn't know how she knew, she just did, and his actions did nothing to deny her fear.

He helped her to their bedroom and to their bed, stripping her and changing her into her nightgown, and then he went into the living room, returning sometime later that night.

Allie had lain awake the whole time, trying unsuccessfully to sleep and block out the gouging pain. Now she and Corliss lay side by side, the physical distance between them nothing compared to the emotional gulf.

"Why did you do it, Allie?" Corliss whispered.

Allie squeezed her eyes shut, and then they popped open. At first she thought he was referring to the fact that she had waited so long to get prenatal care, but something in his tone made her realize he meant something else.

"What did the nurse tell you when she called?" she asked.

"She said you needed picked up after your procedure." He ground his fists into his eyes, making her realize he was crying—the first time she had ever seen him cry. "She tried to make it sound so clinical and professional, but I've heard the euphemisms before. It doesn't sound any better by calling it a procedure instead of an abortion. You could have given it to me. I would have raised it by myself."

Until then, Allie hadn't known her pain could go any deeper. Then she realized her husband thought she went behind his back and got rid of their baby, and her already shredded psyche took another crippling blow, one from which she could never recover. She wanted to defend herself, but the fear that he wouldn't believe her ran too deep. After all, hadn't she been the one to insist she still had choices? Hadn't she lamented her pregnancy on an almost daily basis? A part of her couldn't fault him for thinking so ill of her, but the other part, the emotional part that was still reeling from loss, couldn't forgive him for his calloused indifference to her pain.

She rolled away from him, facing the wall and thinking.

In the morning, she was still in pain, both physically and emotionally. For the first time, she skipped school. Corliss brought her a tray of breakfast, along with her medication, and then he left the apartment. When he returned late that afternoon, he found his bags packed and sitting in the living room, along with Allie, sitting pale and drawn on the couch.

"What's this?" he asked, motioning toward his bags.

"You can't stay here anymore," she said blankly.

He stared at her, his expression equally as empty. "Is this really what you want?"

No, *she thought.* I want you to know me well enough to realize I would never have done what you thought I did. I want you to love me and comfort me and tell me we'll get through this. I want you to tell me we'll try again when we're ready. *"Yes, this is what I want. I want to focus on my career."*

He sneered then, and the sight of his disdain cut through her like a knife. "I knew you were ambitious, Allie, but this..." He broke off and shook his head. "I had no idea you were as cold hearted as this. I hope your precious career will keep you warm at night." With that, he had gathered his bags and walked out the door.

CHAPTER 15

*I*n the morning, they woke at the same time, still stuck together as if they had been glued that way. Corliss brushed Allie's hair from her face and they stared at each other, warily, as if waiting to see what the other would do.

Allie wondered if Corliss remembered the significance of the day. Did it mean anything to him that on this day five years ago she had lost their baby? Did he remember? If the searing intensity in his pain-filled gaze was any indication, then the answer was yes.

Unable to bear his scrutiny any longer, she tried to turn away, but he held her back.

"Don't," he said, practically choking on the word. "Can't you see how much I need you, Allie?"

"Corliss," she breathed, tipping her face up for a kiss.

When he tried to kiss her and couldn't, he groaned in frustration. "Stupid broken jaw," he muttered, causing Allie to laugh.

"Don't laugh," he said. "This is horrible. Who knew I would want to do something even more than I want to eat?"

Her smile flitted away as the tension settled between them again. "Maybe you can't kiss me, but I can kiss you," she said, reaching up to capture any part of him she could reach. He pulled her closer, shuddering, and a couple of minutes later she pulled herself away, sitting up.

"What? What is it?" he asked, sitting up, too.

"The doorbell is ringing," she said.

"It is?" he asked. "I thought that sound was in my head." Now that they were both paying attention, they heard not only the doorbell ringing insistently, but urgent pounding, as if someone was fleeing for his life.

"If that's your cop friend, I won't be held responsible for my actions."

She smiled, leaning forward on her knees to kiss the tip of his nose. "I'll go make sure it's not a life or death situation and get rid of whoever it is." She darted off the bed and grabbed her robe as Corliss practically fell out of bed in his haste to stop her.

"No, Allie, don't answer…" he called, but it was too late. She flung the door open, too muddled to even look through the peephole.

"Brent," she exclaimed as her brother-in-law practically fell into the door.

"Brent," Corliss echoed, exiting the bedroom hopping on one foot as he tried to put on pants. "What are you doing here?"

It was the first time Allie had ever heard Corliss close to sounding impatient with one of his brothers.

"It's Haley," Brent said, collapsing on the couch. Corliss and Allie sat on either side of him, darting looks of concern over his bent head. Brent wasn't one to fall apart, and now he looked not merely disheveled, but wild.

"What about her?" Corliss asked.

"She's gone," Brent said, running his hands through his hair and grasping it at the roots.

"What do you mean gone?" Allie said.

"I mean gone. She cleared out her apartment, she closed her credit and phone accounts, and she cleared out her bank account."

Allie gasped and Corliss's brow lowered. "She took the money?" he said.

Brent nodded. "But I don't care about the money; it was hers to take. I want to know where she is and if she's okay. She's so little and innocent. What if something's happened to her? What if someone is hurting her?"

Allie laid a comforting hand on his back, patting him gently to try and get him to calm down. In eleven years, she had never seen any of the Honeywells fall apart as Brent was now.

"What am I going to do?" Brent asked. He sounded as wretched as he looked.

Corliss scrunched his brow, speaking slowly and carefully. "Well, maybe you should let her go."

"What?" Brent and Allie said together, both looking at him.

He shrugged. "It certainly seems like she doesn't want to be found. Taking the money is pretty final."

"Maybe," Brent said uncertainly, dropping his head in his hands once more.

"Corliss," Allie snapped. "What is wrong with you? That's horrible advice." She gave Brent's shoulders a shake. "Do you love her, Brent?"

"I…" He broke off and looked up, staring at Allie. "She's twenty," he mumbled.

"If she were thirty, would you love her?"

"Of course I would," he said vehemently.

"If she were twenty five, would you love her?"

He nodded.

"If she were twenty two and out of college, would you love her?"

He cast his eyes heavenward, considering. "Yes."

She paused, letting the idea she had planted take root before she spoke. "Then what difference does a couple of years make?" she asked at last.

"Not a whole hill-of-beans lot," Brent said at last. He drew a shaky breath and let it out slowly. "But what if Corliss is right? What if this is her way of telling me she doesn't want to be found? I mean, her note said as much."

"Let me tell you something, little sister to big brother: when a woman says 'don't find me,' it usually means, 'whatever you do, please come find me.' If you love her, really love her, then don't let anything stop you until you find her. And then, when you find her, you can ask her in person if she wants you to go."

"What if she says yes?" Brent asked.

"Don't believe her." She gave his shoulders a squeeze. "You're a Honeywell. Since when do y'all take no for an answer?"

He smiled slightly for the first time since he arrived. "I don't know where to begin," he said, sounding almost shy for the first time since she'd known him.

"Corliss knows a private investigator. Try there," she said. She gave his shoulders another squeeze. "Want some breakfast?"

He nodded, swiping at his nose and looking more like a ten-year-old boy than a thirty-two-year-old man.

"What are we having?" he asked.

"That's up to your brother," she said.

Brent darted Corliss a look. "You cook?"

"Only in Chicago," Corliss replied with a smile, but the humor didn't quite reach his eyes. Instead, he regarded Allie with a studying gaze that made her squirm under his scrutiny. What did he think when he looked at her that way? Was he reliving the past half hour in their room, or the past five years they'd lived apart?

"So what's been going on with you, sugar?" Brent asked as he and Allie sat in the small kitchen and watched Corliss cook.

"Nothing much. Corliss got shot yesterday."

"Where at?" Brent asked, his tone casual as he sipped his coffee. Only a Honeywell would meet the information that a family member had been shot with such a blasé attitude, in Allie's opinion.

"On the sidewalk," Corliss said, and that was the end of that conversation.

"This is a real cute place you have here," Brent said, looking around. "Sorry I never made it here, er, before."

"That's okay," Allie assured him, trying to smooth over any awkwardness the comment had caused. "I'm glad you're here now, even if it's under unfortunate circumstances." She smiled, realizing how much she meant it. All the brothers were close, but at ten months apart, Brent and Corliss were more like twins.

"What happens now?" Brent asked, looking between Allie and Corliss. They froze, looking at anything but each other. "In the investigation," Brent added hastily, and they relaxed.

"It's in the hands of some officer who has a fierce crush on Allie," Corliss said disdainfully.

"Corliss," Allie exclaimed, embarrassed.

"What are you going to do about it?" Brent asked.

"I hired my own investigator," Corliss replied.

Brent nodded approvingly as if that had been the most obvious course of action. "What can I do?" he asked.

Allie crossed her fingers that Brent wouldn't also come to work with her the next day, but when Corliss spoke, she thought work might be a preferable solution.

"You can come with me while I interview some people."

Allie sat up in alarm. "What people?"

"Some people involved in the dead judge case."

"Corliss, you can't."

"I can and I will, Allie," he said.

"You can't harass the people involved in that case. And, besides, that family is filled with thugs who have suspected mob ties."

"All the more reason to get some answers to my questions," Corliss said.

"But," Allie tried, but he interrupted her with a shake of his head. "I'm a private citizen," he said soothingly. "I can have a friendly chat with whomever I want."

Despite the fact that Allie had spent several years training in rhetoric and persuasion, she gave up trying to sway him. Long ago she had learned to recognize when debate was futile with Corliss. In fact, looking for that same stubborn expression on a potential juror's face had probably saved her from a few dozen trial losses. Never selecting jurors who reminded her of Corliss had become her touchstone in more ways than one.

After a breakfast of bread pudding with caramel sauce and grilled peaches, Allie cleaned up the kitchen while the brothers sat at the table and talked. When Brent excused himself, Corliss came up to stand behind her, tentatively slipping his arms around her waist. She leaned her back against him with the same sort of hesitancy. Both of them felt like they were walking through a minefield in some ways and unwilling to disturb the new peace between them.

"Thanks for cleaning up," he murmured, leaning forward to press his lips to her neck.

"Thanks for making breakfast. I think you might be my favorite cook."

"Better than your mom?" he asked, smiling.

"It's been so long since I had her cooking, I don't remember."

"Me too," he said, and they shared a laugh.

"I'll talk to Mom and tell her to back off," Allie volunteered.

"She warned me about coming here," he said. "She told me if I hurt you again, she'll leave."

She stiffened slightly and swallowed hard. "Don't hurt me, Corliss," she said, half teasing and half pleading.

"Don't hurt me, Allie," he added in the same tone. He gave her waist a squeeze and kissed her cheek, letting her go when Brent returned.

Since Brent had never been to Chicago, they took him to see the sights. After supper at a steakhouse—where Corliss ate soup and mashed potatoes—they went to see the Royal Lipizzaner Stallions who happened to be in town for the weekend. The show was spectacular, but their little party was subdued. Though Brent put on a happy face, he was still clearly upset about Haley. And though Allie and Corliss tried to be similarly upbeat, there was still tension humming between them, stilting their conversations.

They returned to the apartment and turned on a movie, the same one they'd been trying unsuccessfully to watch for the past few nights. Brent sat on one end, vaguely paying attention but clearly distracted, while Allie and Corliss sat on the other end, showing more interest in each other than in the movie.

Allie couldn't help feeling like she was sixteen all over again. Corliss sat beside her, his hand resting a few inches away but seemingly out of reach. She wasn't sure they had ever been so hesitant with each other, but neither wanted to make the wrong move. How could someone be so familiar to her, and yet so new? And he was her husband, no less. She shouldn't feel awkward with him. She never had before, and she didn't like the feeling now.

At last she screwed up her courage and made the first move, sliding closer to him until she was pressed against his side. He reciprocated by resting his hand on her leg and giving it a gentle squeeze.

By the time the movie finished, they were all blinking sleepily, but Allie found she wasn't ready to go into the bedroom. While she and Corliss had found a small measure of comfort with each other on the couch, going to their room felt like starting all over again. But Brent was clearly exhausted. Allie made up a bed for him on the couch, lamenting his large size and the couch's smallness, but he didn't seem concerned by the fact that he was practically folded in half.

"Don't trouble yourself, sugar. If I really minded where I slept, I would get a hotel," he assured her with a friendly squeeze of her bicep.

When his bed was arranged and she could think of no more excuses to remain in the living room, she plodded toward the bedroom. Corliss was already in bed, staring intently at the ceiling like it held the answers to life's greatest questions.

Allie took her time in the bathroom, half hoping Corliss would be asleep when she emerged. But he wasn't. He remained staring at the ceiling and she had to glance at him a couple of times to make sure he was blinking.

She crawled under the covers, turned out her bedside lamp, and did some ceiling staring of her own. There was a foot between them, and the tension was oppressive. Neither of them spoke for so long that Allie was sure he was asleep, and then he finally whispered her name.

"Allie."

"What?" she whispered.

He nervously cleared his throat. "Where, um, where did we leave off this morning?"

She smiled. Never in eleven years had she heard Corliss nervous before, not even on their wedding night, and the sound did something to her heart, softening her resolve where she once might have remained resolute and followed her logic, the logic that told her not to get too close to him yet. Instead she turned off her brain and rolled over, propping herself on his chest.

"Right about here, I think," she said, and then she kissed him.

CHAPTER 16

The next morning, they lay together, talking softly.

"I wish I didn't have to go to work," Allie said. "I wish I could stay like this all day."

"Can't you? Take a day off. Goodness knows after being shot at, you've earned it."

"I can't. I have court today. Plus, it might be sort of awkward for us to remain in our room all day while your brother is here."

"Brent's so heartbroken, I'm not sure he'd notice."

They both frowned as they stared thoughtfully at the far wall. He didn't like to see Brent upset, and she didn't like to see Corliss upset because Brent was upset.

"It doesn't sound like there's an easy solution to the Brent/Haley situation," she commented.

"Is there ever an easy solution for anyone?" Corliss asked. "'The course of true love never did run smooth,' after all."

She rolled over to smile up at him. "Look at you, quoting Shakespeare when there's nothing I can do about it."

"And look at you, so pretty in the morning when there's nothing I can do about it." He smoothed his hand gently over her hair, smiling as best he could. "I've missed you, Allie. I've missed this."

"Me, too," she agreed, not sure why she was whispering except that the moment seemed sacred somehow. They looked at each other awhile longer, allowing physical touch to heal things their words couldn't, and then she kissed him and slipped out of bed. Since she had lingered so long, she had to hurry to make it on time. She intended to skip breakfast, but Corliss forced a glass of juice down her and shoved a travel mug of coffee in her hand, and then they were off.

Allie felt very much like the middle of an M as she walked between the two brothers. They towered over her so that even more people turned to stare at her today than they had when Corliss escorted her to work. Today he took her to the courthouse, smiling as he glanced at her suit, glasses, and professional-looking French twist.

"You look very studious," he said.

"You'd be surprised how much my appearance plays a role in the jury's decision," she said. "If I look smart and capable, they're more apt to believe me."

"Good thing for me you actually are smart and capable," he said, pausing outside the entrance of her courtroom. He tipped her chin up and gave her a brief peck on the lips. The kiss wasn't scandalous or intimate, but Allie felt it all the way to her toes.

"Don't go anywhere alone," Corliss warned. "Not even to the bathroom. I wouldn't be leaving you today if it wasn't important."

"This is a courthouse with armed guards," she assured him. "I'll be fine." When he still looked reluctant to leave her, she patted his bicep and waved him away with a smile. "Have fun with your brother. I think he needs some cheering up or distracting." They both turned to look at Brent who stared dismally into space.

"I guess it's my turn to do some cheering," Corliss said cryptically, making her wonder what condition he had been in five years ago when they separated. He squeezed her hand and she watched him walk away, her heart turning somersaults like it had when she was a kid and so in love with someone who was so out of reach. With a decisive shake of her head, she forced Corliss from her mind and turned her thoughts to work.

Corliss, on the other hand, had no luck getting Allie off his mind.

It didn't help that Brent was uncharacteristically silent and sullen, at least until they reached the car.

"Looks like things are going well between you and Allie," he commented.

"Yeah, I guess so," Corliss said uncertainly.

"That doesn't sound convincing," Brent said.

Corliss sighed. "They are and they aren't. We're enjoying being with each other, but we haven't talked about anything. And you remember yesterday when she said that when a woman says to leave she doesn't mean it? Those are almost the same words she said to me five years ago. I can't help but wonder if, when she told me to leave, what she really meant was to stay. What if I've stayed away all this time when what she really wanted was for me to be here, fighting for her?"

"Do you want to fight for her? Some bad things passed between you," Brent said.

Corliss hissed a breath between his teeth. "I don't know. I love her, you know that, but I'm not sure I can forgive her for what she did." He frowned. "It's still so unlike her. Back then, Allie was so uncertain of herself and her identity as my wife that she barely bought postage stamps without running it by me first. It's hard to reconcile she did what she did without even talking it over with me."

"You said she was under a lot of strain," Brent said. "Stress can have adverse effects on people's behavior. They pull up stakes and flee across the country, for instance." He crossed his arms over his chest and turned to stare out the window. They rode in silence for a while as they each brooded, and then Brent spoke again. "I'm not very astute when it comes to women, but I've learned something recently; they don't think normal."

"Tell me about it," Corliss said.

"No, I mean it," Brent continued, impassioned now. "All this time I thought there was a chance Haley had a crush on me, but she never came out and said anything. And all this time I thought she blamed me for killing her dad, but she never did. How could I have gotten everything so wrong?"

"I don't know," Corliss said thoughtfully. "Do you think maybe there's something wrong with us that the women in our lives ran away or threw us out?"

They were quiet a few minutes as they thought that over.

"Nah," they said together, and that was the end of the discussion.

It took awhile to find the person they were looking for. Corliss had to grease a few palms with money before anyone would talk and tell him where to find Jimmy DeSant, Jr., the son of the man Allie convicted in the trial she shared with the deceased judge. Finally they tracked him down at a seedy-looking bar at which, under normal circumstances, neither of the brothers would be caught dead.

"Are you Jimmy DeSant?" Corliss asked when they approached a weasel-faced, greasy little man nursing a beer at the bar.

"Who wants to know?" the man asked sullenly, then flinched in surprise when he looked up to see Corliss and Brent towering over him.

"I do," Corliss said.

Jimmy swallowed hard. "Fine. I'm Jimmy. What's it to you?"

Corliss sat on one side of him and Brent sat on the other. Jimmy twisted to look nervously between them. "I want to talk about your father's case," Corliss said.

Jimmy scowled. "What of it? He didn't do nothin' they said he did."

"I'm sure he was an innocent paragon of virtue," Brent said sarcastically. On the way, Corliss had filled him in on Jimmy Sr.'s many crimes.

"Maybe he wasn't no saint, but he didn't deserve what that witch did to him on the stand," Jimmy said.

"That witch being the prosecutor, Allison Honeywell?"

Jimmy frowned. "I thought her name was Miller."

"It's Miller-Honeywell," Corliss corrected. "What exactly did she do to him?"

"She got him all mixed up on the witness stand until he started admitting to stuff he didn't do. That witch is the reason he's in jail," he said bitterly.

Corliss could have commented on the fact that, by being cleverer than his father, Allie had gotten the man to admit to his crimes on the witness stand. That it wasn't Allie who had committed the crimes in the first place, nor made the arrest. But he didn't. He wasn't concerned with any of that today.

"And that made you angry, huh?" he asked, his tone sympathetic.

"Of course it did," Jimmy said, angrily slamming his beer on the bar so that some of it sloshed over the side. "Someone needs to teach that witch a lesson."

"Someone like you?" Corliss asked casually.

Jimmy opened his mouth to reply before casting Corliss another suspicious look. "Who did you say you are?"

"I didn't," Corliss said. "You were telling me how much you hate Ms. Honeywell and how much you hope she gets what's coming to her," he prompted.

"Well, she does have it coming, but I ain't never done nothing to no woman, and especially not a fed."

Allie wasn't a federal prosecutor, but Corliss got the gist of what Jimmy was trying to say. "Are you sure, Jimmy? Are you sure you didn't try to take her down on Saturday evening?"

Jimmy paled, looking between Corliss and Brent again. "What? I didn't...I never...Look, I was at the races all evening on Saturday. You can ask anyone."

"What about someone you know, someone who owes you a favor? Might they take down Allie for you as an act of kindness?"

"No," Jimmy said vehemently. "Look, I swear it. I might, you know, bend the law a little here and there, but I'm not stupid enough to try and kill a prosecutor, and especially not a woman."

"Do you know anyone who might be that stupid?" Corliss asked.

Jimmy cast his eyes heavenward, thinking, and then he shrugged. "I dunno. Could be anyone. The witch has made a lot of enemies." He looked at Corliss again. "What's it to you anyway?"

"The witch is my wife," Corliss said, standing. Jimmy flinched away from him, but Corliss had no desire to waste his energy on the stupid little man. He and Brent left the bar as quietly as they had entered.

"What do you think?" Corliss asked when they reached the car. "Do you think he was telling the truth?"

"I think he's too dumb, weak, and cowardly to know which end of the gun is backward," Brent said. "He's all talk."

"I got that impression, too," Corliss said, although he didn't sound happy about it. "I have no idea where to go from here. He was my only lead."

Brent stared thoughtfully through the front windshield for a while. "You said she and the judge had worked a previous case together. Was he assigned to any of her upcoming cases?"

Corliss stirred restlessly in his seat. "That's a good idea. I'll have to look into it tomorrow when she's back at the office."

"Let's go to court so I can live vicariously through my little sister-in-law," Brent suggested.

"Do you ever regret not going into trial law?" Corliss asked.

"Sometimes, but, you know."

Corliss nodded. He did know. It was a foregone conclusion that all of the sons would give up any outside career ambitions in order to devote themselves to the farm. And none of them resented it because their parents had given so much and asked so little in return. In fact, they hadn't even mandated that their sons take over the horse farm; it was a foregone conclusion in the brothers' minds that none of them would leave. Only Ivy was free to go away and have the life she wanted.

They slipped into the back of the courtroom if not unnoticed then at least without making a scene. Allie was still examining Mr. Pratt who was still surly. Corliss began to see why Jimmy DeSant was so angry with her. She was relentless, not allowing the hapless Mr. Pratt an instant to compose himself between her verbal parries. She was like a cobra, striking again and again until at last Mr. Pratt broke down and began weeping.

Corliss shouldn't have found her so attractive then, but he did. The fact that he was one of only a handful of people who knew her vulnerable soft side went straight to his head, making him almost crazy in love with her.

Mr. Pratt's attorney asked for another recess and the judge adjourned court for the day. Allie turned from the witness stand. Corliss caught her eye and winked, and she gave him a small smile before gathering her briefcase.

People stood and began filing out of the courtroom. Beside Corliss, Brent sat smiling proudly. "She's a little firecracker, isn't she? Did you see the way she ripped into that guy? I would guess that's the first time he's cried since he became a grownup." He paused. "Maybe he's the one who's trying to kill her."

"I'm convinced they all want to kill her," Corliss said. "In the last two years, she's handled over five hundred cases. That's five hundred Jimmys and Mr. Pratts. Her enemy list is endless."

"Maybe it's time to pack it in and bring her back to Kentucky," Brent suggested.

"Did you see her?" Corliss asked. "This is what she wants to do. She's given up everything for her career, and she's good at it." He shook his head. "Trying to argue with her and make her do something she doesn't want to do doesn't work. Long ago I learned to simply get on board and support her when I know there's no changing her mind." He had tried once, to change her mind when it didn't want to be changed, and it had ended in the loss of their child. *Never again,* he promised himself. If he and Allie couldn't come to some type of peaceable resolution, then they would go their separate ways again. Better that than dragging her back to Kentucky and trying to fit her into his mold.

"Good job, sugar," Brent said, cajoling Corliss out of his wayward thoughts. He watched as his brother gave Allie's shoulders a companionable squeeze and she patted his chest in return. The little piece of Corliss's heart that had been out of sync popped into place at having the people he loved most together again. Nothing, no matter how good, had felt right without Allie. And without her continued presence in his life, nothing would feel right again. But how to make her stay? That was the question he had to figure out an answer to, the sooner, the better.

CHAPTER 17

"It was nice to see Brent again."

"Mmm, hmm," Corliss answered absently.

Allie smiled, thinking of Corliss's brothers. For some reason, even though she and Ivy were the same age, they had never been close. She had been much closer to the brothers, claiming them as her own. Maybe it was because Ivy was always so soft, sweet, gentle, and feminine. Her blond-haired, blue-eyed beauty had made her seem remote somehow, even though Allie knew she was perfectly friendly. Still, she had intimidated Allie who never seemed to be able to resist a fight or keep her mouth shut when she disagreed with an opinion. The brothers, who all suffered the same problem, had been easy to be around because she never had to keep a muzzle on her mouth. Plus, Corliss was always with his brothers, and Allie had been wherever Corliss was.

"We're being followed again," Corliss announced abruptly, shattering the pleasant silence.

"Are you sure?" Allie asked. She didn't really doubt him, but she was in shock. Things had been so pleasant the last couple of days; she had begun to forget the ugliness of the threats and shooting.

"I'm sure," Corliss replied. "I think it's the same car. Where's the nearest police station?"

She told him, and he headed there, the car staying on their tail until they arrived. Corliss pulled into the lot and parked. "Come on," he said. "I want to make a report."

"Corliss, it won't do any good," she said.

"I don't care, Allie. There needs to be a record of this. Aren't you the one who is always telling me a paper trail is important? What if, when they catch this guy, they can match the description of his car to this report?"

"It won't do any good, Corliss. It won't add anything to the charges. All it will do is waste our time."

He banged his fist on the steering wheel, startling her. "This is crazy. Can't you see how crazy this is? You're being stalked by a potential killer and yet you say the police can't help you. Twice now you've been followed and someone shot at you."

She sighed. "What do you expect me to do about it, Corliss?"

"I expect you to take a few days off and get out of town until this blows over."

"I can't do that," she said without even thinking about it. "Especially not in the middle of the Pratt case. It's going to be hard enough to try and get a murder conviction without a body. I have a good momentum going, and if I leave, I'm going to lose that. I know that probably doesn't make sense to you, but jurors are fickle. Everything I can do to nudge them in the way I want them to go helps."

"Do you hear yourself? You've lost everything else, but is your career more important than your life? Because that's what it sounds like to me."

Her eyes rounded with pain. "Low blow, Corliss."

They sat in heavy silence for a few minutes, trying to cool off. Eventually Corliss started the car. She thought they were going home, but he surprised her by pulling in front of a shady-looking gun store.

"Come on," he said.

"What are we doing here?"

"The three day waiting period is up and our permits are valid. We're picking up our guns."

"Corliss," she started, but he shook his head.

"Don't start with me, Allie." He came around to her side of the car and held her door, walking quietly along beside her as they entered the store. She hovered near the door, feeling uncomfortable, as Corliss paid for their guns and another curious object that looked like an antennae attached to a metal disc.

When they left the store, he grasped her forearm to hold her back while he extended the antennae. She realized it was a telescoping mirror and tried not to roll her eyes as he used it to look under the car for bombs. Apparently he had missed his calling as James Bond.

The ride back to their apartment was similarly quiet, though Corliss politely held her doors for her as if nothing were amiss. She would have gone straight to bed without saying a word, but as soon as he removed his shirt, she remembered the wound on his shoulder needed cleaned and dressed.

"Sit," she commanded, pointing to the toilet.

"Yes, ma'am," he said meekly, then winced when she mercilessly ripped off his bandage.

"It hurts less if you do it all at once," she said.

"If you say so."

While she was busy working on his shoulder, Corliss was similarly busy working on her, his hands skimming her back, waist, legs, and anywhere else he could reach.

"Stop it, Corliss," she snapped, trying in vain to move away from his wandering hands.

"Why?" he said.

"Because I'm mad at you," she said.

"Why?" he asked.

"Because…well…I don't remember, but I'm sure it was a valid reason."

"Not as valid as the reason I have for wanting to touch you," he said.

"And what's that?" she asked, smiling despite her best efforts not to.

"You're pretty, and soft, and I've gone for five years without you, and I don't want to go another day."

She pressed his bandage into place, sealing the edges before answering. "All right, you win; your reason is better," she said. Leaning down to cup his face in her hands, she kissed him. And when he carried her from the room, she didn't object at all.

For the next couple of days, Corliss and Allie settled into the comfortable routine they had adapted when they lived together before their separation. The only difference was that now Corliss came to work with her, reviewing her old and new cases while she worked.

He had discovered two upcoming cases the deceased judged had been assigned to preside over. He poured over them obsessively, going over and over the witness list and evidence until he felt like Allie's second chair. While everyone involved had motive, no one person had more motive than anyone else. Corliss was frustrated, and he couldn't shake the feeling that he was missing something glaringly obvious, though he had no idea what it might be. It would be helpful to talk to the detective in charge of Allie's case, but since that was Marlin, Corliss didn't see that happening any time soon. To make matters worse, Marlin refused to share his information with the private investigator, meaning the investigator had to start from scratch—probably duplicating everything the detective had already done.

Corliss wanted to share his concerns with Allie, but didn't want to disturb the easy peace that had settled between them. Especially because she bristled at any mention of Marlin, as if Corliss were casting doubt on her judgment instead of the detective's.

As for Allie, she was feeling positively spoiled by Corliss. In the evenings, he cooked for them, and it was always delicious. She could feel herself gaining weight, but lacked the will to care. The last few years had been an odd time where she usually felt too tired, too stressed, or too sad to eat. Rounding out her figure right now was a good thing.

After supper, they cleaned the kitchen together and retreated to the couch, lying on opposite ends and reading their respective books. Before Corliss came back, Allie had lived on a steady diet of current bestsellers, at least whenever she had the chance to read. But now, with his literary influence as a guide, she was rereading the classics and realizing how much she had missed them. Nothing like a little *Jane Eyre* to make her present circumstances look less gloomy.

All in all, they were like any happily married couple, except they hadn't spoken of the five years they spent apart or the reason for their separation. Allie felt like they were carefully tiptoeing around the subject. Whether it was because they wanted to lay a groundwork of emotional and physical connection before they tackled it or because they were afraid to ruin what they now had, she didn't know. And she didn't care. For now, Corliss was here, and he showed no intentions of going away. As long as they could maintain the status quo, she was happy.

But of course the status quo was impossible to maintain. Even if they might have been able to keep up the loving happiness between them, outside forces were bound to intrude, which they did one night after supper when Allie's phone rang. She answered sleepily, reluctantly drawing her attention from Corliss who had been massaging her feet and calves one-handed while he read his book. When she sat up in alarm and answered in short, one-word sentences, Corliss set aside his book and tensed, waiting to see what the problem was.

"Yes, yes, I'll do that. Okay. Goodbye," she said, closing her phone and setting it aside.

"What is it?" Corliss asked. "Allie," he added, tapping her shin when she remained staring into space.

"That was an officer from South Chicago. They found the body of Jimmy DeSant, Jr. Marlin is handling the case because of the connection to the judge, and he wants to talk to you." She bit her lip and looked at Corliss. "I think you should get a lawyer."

"Why? I didn't do anything wrong."

"Believe me when I tell you that guilt or innocence doesn't matter much in the hands of a skilled detective."

"I'll take my chances," Corliss said, stirring from his comfortable position on the couch. "Let's go."

CHAPTER 18

*A*llie felt a bit surreal as she and Corliss sat in the small interrogation room with Marlin across the desk from them. Her first instinct was to think like Marlin and try to figure out if Corliss was guilty. But since she knew Corliss was innocent, she had to force herself to think like a defense attorney and try to keep him from saying anything that might incriminate himself, especially because he adamantly refused to hire an actual defense attorney. On top of all that, Marlin was extremely unhappy about having her in the room, citing conflict of interest as his main concern. Corliss had made clear his opinion on Marlin's opinion—that he shouldn't have an opinion where his wife was concerned—and the tension in the room was now at the boiling point.

"Let's go over this again," Marlin said for the fifth time. He was using a tactic Allie knew well, trying to trip Corliss up by rehashing the story. He was also using time as a weapon. It was nearing midnight, and they were all exhausted. Corliss, however, was proving to be an excellent suspect, at least from a defense attorney's point of view. He hadn't changed his story, hadn't become confused, and hadn't become tired, all of which were proving to make Marlin more frustrated than Corliss. "You went to see Jimmy DeSant at Mick's bar, his usual hangout."

"That's correct," Corliss replied. "My brother was with me. We had a pleasant conversation and we left. That was the last time I ever saw him."

"You had a pleasant conversation with Jimmy DeSant," Marlin said skeptically. "The man never had a pleasant conversation with anyone in his life."

"Maybe you simply had to know how to talk to him. Whatever the reason, I asked him a couple of questions, got the answers I needed, and left the bar."

"You got answers from Jimmy DeSant," Marlin said. "What did that cost you?"

"A few minutes of my time," Corliss said. "I found him ready and willing to answer any questions I had about Allie. For some reason, he didn't much care for her." He turned to give Allie a look and a small smile.

"Do you think this is funny, Mr. Honeywell?" Marlin snapped.

Corliss's smile faded and he turned to look at Marlin with a scorching glare. "Do I think it's funny that a man is dead? No. Do I think it's funny that I'm a suspect in his murder? No. Do I think it's funny that the officer assigned to the case is biased by his feelings for my wife? No. Do I think it's funny that your conduct is unprofessional? No. Does that answer your question, Detective?"

"Unprofessional?" Marlin thundered, slapping his palms on the table. "I resent the accusation."

"I resent this entire process," Corliss yelled. "I'm doing my best to make sure Allie's safe and, though you say you share that goal, you won't help me."

"I don't owe you or your investigator anything. I don't want a couple of amateurs screwing up my investigation."

Both men had leaned forward, breathing hard like raging bulls about to take a run at each other. Allie cleared her throat and they turned to look at her. "Gentlemen, are we done here?" she said calmly, trying to restore some sense of reason to the small space.

"No," Marlin said. "I have more questions."

It was time for Allie to put her foot down. "Marlin, either charge him or let him go. Our cooperation is at an end; Corliss has answered all of your questions. You don't have any evidence to charge him, and you know it. Not least of which because he's been with me every minute since he arrived here, and especially at the time of the murder. I think you'll find it very hard to make a murder charge stick with a prosecuting attorney as an alibi."

"You're biased, Allison," Marlin said softly. "You can't see the truth about him."

"The truth is that he's my husband, and he didn't commit this murder. And I would hope that after so many years of working together you would realize that if I thought he had murdered someone, I would be the first one to put the cuffs on him, marriage vows or not." She stood. "We're done here."

Corliss stood and followed her from the room, wisely remaining silent and keeping his eyes on her instead of on the detective. If he looked at the man and saw another expression of love on his face when he looked at Allie, he wouldn't be held responsible for his actions.

"I think that went well," he said as they reached their car. He held Allie back while he checked underneath with the telescoping mirror, squinting to see in the dim parking garage.

"Mmm, hmm," she said absently.

"Are you okay?" he asked, noting her stilted tone. He opened her door and she waited to speak until he slid behind the wheel.

"I feel horrible about this whole situation," she said.

"Why? You had nothing to do with Jimmy DeSant's death."

"Not that, though it is horrible. I'm talking about you."

"What about me?" he asked.

"I've ripped you away from your peaceful Kentucky home and dropped you into the middle of Chicago where you get shot at and become the suspect in a murder." She sighed, leaning against the seat and closing her eyes.

Corliss rested his hand on her knee and gave it a gentle squeeze.

"Allie, we're married. It's probably about time I started using those vows we took. Your life is mine, and vice versa. Maybe..." he paused, gathering courage. "Maybe when this is all over you could take some time off and visit the farm. A little time in the country might do you good."

"That sounds nice," she said, trying to imagine a scenario when she could ever actually take a vacation. Seeing her mother and his family and the beautiful farm where she had spent so much of her adolescence did sound ideal, though, and she found herself almost yearning for the privilege. Since he had tentatively approached the subject of "them," she decided to take a stab at it, too.

"Corliss, how long are you going to stay?"

He darted a look at her before turning back to the road. "Ready for me to leave?"

"Of course not," she said earnestly, covering his hand with hers. "It's that I know you've left your family in the lurch, and I feel bad about that." *And I'm also beginning to wonder where this is headed. Oh, and I'm falling more in love with you than ever and truly might die when you leave.*

"Don't worry about it, Allie," he said.

She faced forward with a dissatisfied frown. Don't worry about what? The fact that he had left a gaping hole in his family's horse business? Or the fact that she had no idea what their future held? Or maybe she shouldn't worry about the fact that they still hadn't discussed their past. Or was he telling her not to worry about the fact that someone was trying to kill her and they had no leads. There was so much she *shouldn't* worry about that she was overwhelmed.

"Does your investigator have any leads?" she asked. Someone was trying to kill her, and it was a sad testament to the state of her life that it was the least of her worries.

"No," Corliss said, sounding weary. He turned his head slightly in her direction and gave her a wry smile. "Do you have any idea how many people want to kill you?"

"A lot, I suppose," she said, sounding dismal.

"If I had known how unpopular you were going to be..." He let the words trail off as he arrived at a stop sign and looked back and forth to make sure no cars were coming.

"Then what?" she asked tersely.

"Then I'd have married you anyway." Smiling, he leaned over the console and kissed her. He couldn't really kiss her with his mouth wired shut as it was, but he did a good job considering what he had to work with, good enough that she reached for him, forgetting they were in a car in the middle of an intersection until the car behind them honked.

The car took off again, and Allie sat back, thinking. If she knew how painful their marriage was going to be before she married him, would she still have married him? Had it been worth it? Did the happiness outweigh the pain and separation?

Yes, she realized. Painful as it sometimes was, she would still hitch her wagon to Corliss Honeywell. And maybe there was hope for their future. True, they still hadn't broached the painful subjects between them, but they were together and they were happy, weren't they? And didn't the fact that they hadn't divorced say something about their commitment to each other? Or was it a testament to their laziness? Divorce wasn't for slouches. There was a lot of legal backbending. Was the reason he hadn't asked for one due to the fact that it hadn't been worth the hassle? Was it easier to live apart and pretend he hadn't been married rather than to seek a divorce and pick his way through the legal red tape? She wanted to ask him but, as with everything else between them, she was afraid.

They finished the ride in silence and fell into bed exhausted. Allie's normal wakeup time rolled around too early, and they lay in bed, trying to put off the inevitable. At last they rolled out of bed, frantically dashing around as they tried to share the bathroom and get ready at the same time. They laughed as they used the sink together and realized Allie didn't have to duck because Corliss was so much taller.

"Who needs two bathrooms?" Corliss said.

"People with children," Allie said without thinking, but Corliss simply smiled and pressed a kiss to the top of her head. They both skipped breakfast, taking coffee to go, and holding hands as they sprinted to their car. Allie wanted to protest when Corliss once again held her back and checked under the car for a bomb. Thankfully, he did it quickly, not giving her time enough to argue with him.

"You could drop me in front of the building while you park," she suggested. "That might save time."

"No," he said. "I'm not leaving your side until we're safely inside." He looked around, eyes narrowed. "This is a perfect place to ambush someone."

"I think you're becoming paranoid, Corliss."

"Where your safety is concerned, I don't care if I become downright crazy, Allie. I'm not taking any chances."

Allie tried to hear the concern in his tone and not be weighed down by his stifling over protectiveness. After all, he was putting his life on hold to take care of her. Had she even thanked him for that? He found a parking space and, despite the fact that they were running late, she paused, grasping his forearm to hold him back.

"Thanks for coming here, Corliss."

"I haven't always done the best job of being here for you, Allie. I plan to change that."

Her heart fluttered with the implication, but she had no time to stay and hear him expound on his meaning. A fact which he soon pointed out.

"Aren't you going to be late?" he said, squeezing her hand where it rested on his arm.

"Oh, my," she said. She hated to be late for anything, but especially for work. Laughing, he jogged around the car and clasped her hand, pulling her along beside him at a fast trot that left her laughing and breathless, but somehow managed to get her to her desk on time. Bunny popped her head over her cubicle, smiling.

"Looks like things are going well," she commented.

There was no good reply to that, so Allie and Corliss simply smiled, first at her and then at each other. Corliss sat and began plowing through her cases again, hoping to find the elusive something he was missing. Lunchtime arrived, and they had food delivered.

Corliss had deemed that safer than going out to get something, though neither of them liked the fact that they were trapped in her office all day, especially because it was in the middle of a large room and not near any windows.

"Like a rat in a trap," Corliss muttered darkly on more than one occasion.

"You have to work your way up to an office with windows," Allie always reminded him.

Despite the fact that they were exhausted from their short night and stuck inside when the sun was shining, they were having a good day, at least until Marlin approached them. Corliss tensed, but not as much as Allie. Was Corliss going to be arrested in the middle of her office? But, no, Marlin had something else to say. He ignored Corliss and focused on Allie.

"Good news, Allison. A search of Jimmy DeSant's apartment found the same stationary and magazines he had been using to send you the threatening letters. You're safe. And as for you," he turned to pin Corliss with his steely gaze. "You're free to leave. You can go back to wherever it is you came from." He smiled triumphantly once more at Allie, and then he was gone.

CHAPTER 19

"You don't have to do that. It's over."

Allie stood back and watched as Corliss once again checked under her car for a bomb. He closed the telescoping mirror and opened her door without a word.

"I don't like it," he said once they were both inside the car. "It's too easy."

"*Lex parsimoniae,*" Allie said.

"What?" Corliss said.

"*Lex parsimoniae,*" she repeated. "It's Occam's Razor, basically Law School 101, meaning the simplest theory is usually the one that's correct. Jimmy DeSant had a well-known vendetta against me; Jimmy DeSant had incriminating evidence at his home. Case closed."

"Then who killed Jimmy DeSant and why? It certainly wasn't me."

"There were probably as many people who wanted Jimmy dead as want me dead. He wasn't exactly popular. He was a bookie who skimmed money from his clients. Maybe he skimmed money from the wrong person."

Corliss was still shaking his head. "It doesn't feel right."

"Don't take this the wrong way, Corliss, but you aren't exactly an investigator; you're a farrier. Why would any of this feel right to you?

It makes sense to me, and I investigate this kind of stuff every day. Maybe you don't want to believe it's over because now you have no valid reason to stay."

The words tumbled from her mouth unbidden and hung between them like wet laundry on a cold day.

"Is that your subtle way of telling me to go?" he asked at last.

"No," she said. "I like having you here, but I think we're long overdue for a serious conversation."

"Not yet," Corliss replied.

"Corliss," she began, but he interrupted her.

"Let me satisfy myself that it's really over and you're really out of danger. I'll talk to my investigator and make sure all the loose ends are tied up. I'll stay a few more days and shadow you until I'm convinced you're in the clear, and then we'll have all the talks you want, I promise." He turned toward her with an endearingly roguish smile. "Have I ever broken a promise to you?"

Only once, when you walked out my door five years ago. "No," she said because it was what he expected of her and because she didn't feel like fighting. She turned toward her window with a quiet chuckle.

"What?" he asked.

"I argue for a living, and yet I don't like to argue with you because I always lose. It's maddening."

"That's what makes us work, Allie," he said sincerely. "Think how much you would despise being with someone you could railroad."

"I wouldn't mind railroading you every now and again," she said, only half teasing. The remainder of the drive was silent, and then they were home.

"I'll tell you a secret, Allie," Corliss said as soon as he parked. He leaned close, his lips brushing her ear as he whispered. "You had me wrapped around your finger the day we met. You don't even know how whipped I am when it comes to you."

They sat in the car in the parking garage of their apartment building. The darkness around them made the conversation feel more intimate, and when he undid her seatbelt and slipped his arms around her, lifting her into his lap, she felt like they were the only two people on earth.

"Why doesn't it feel that way?" she asked. "Why does it feel like you're always the one in control?"

"Because that's what you need," he said. "And I swore long ago that I would always try to be whatever you need."

She rested her head on his chest, thinking, hating to admit that what he said was probably true. Corliss was the only strong male presence she'd ever had in her life. How embarrassing that she had married a father figure, but it seemed to be the case. She was an alpha female who probably would eat a lesser man for breakfast. Corliss—so comfortable in his identity that he didn't mind being a farrier even though he had the makings of a literature professor—might be the only man on the planet strong enough to handle her without feeling emasculated.

"You know what I regret about us?" he asked. She tipped her head back so she could see him. "I regret that I didn't give in and kiss you when we were younger because now I really want to kiss you, and a couple of kids making out in a car is far less scandalous than a couple of adults doing the same thing." He smoothed her hair off her face, smiling.

"I won't tell if you won't," she said.

His smile widened and he leaned down to kiss her, stopping short of reaching her lips. "Know what's better than being a teenager and making out in a car?" She shook her head. "Being married adults and making out in our apartment." Laughing, they made their way upstairs to their apartment.

The next week was once again idyllic. Allie and Corliss functioned as if there had never been a rift between them. Anytime Allie broached the topic of having a discussion, Corliss put her off. He was still using the excuse of making sure Jimmy DeSant had really been the one sending her messages. Even though she hadn't received any more messages, no one had followed them, and no one else had taken potshots at her, Corliss remained unconvinced. She tried asking him what his investigator had to say about the situation, but he somehow avoided that topic, too.

Allie felt torn. She was enjoying the time with Corliss, but in a way, it didn't feel real. Simmering below the surface was a whole lot of baggage and somehow at some point, it was all going to rise to the surface. She wanted to clear the air between them because there was a little part of her that always felt anxious, as if Corliss was once again going to disappear. In addition to the fact that they hadn't talked about the past, they also hadn't talked about their future. What were they going to do? Was he going to live with her indefinitely? Did he expect her to move back to Kentucky with him? There was a lot they needed to put on the table. Allie determined that Saturday would be the day to have it out.

But when Saturday morning arrived, Corliss diverted her again.

"Let's go away for the night," he suggested as they lay in bed that morning. Allie had been absently tracing his face, trailing her finger through his cheek stubble. He and his brothers could apparently grow facial hair at will, and she had the vague thought that they could make a lot of money being studied by scientists who work on hair-growing formulas.

"Go away?" she repeated dumbly, only half listening.

He propped himself on one elbow, smiling down at her. "Yes. Let's go away to some idyllic little town, get an outrageously expensive hotel room, and never set foot outside it, thereby missing the town entirely. C'mon, we haven't gone anywhere together since our honeymoon."

She wanted to argue, but she couldn't. The look in Corliss's eyes was almost pleading, as if he knew she had been planning to have a talk and was trying desperately to divert her. She sighed. "Okay, we'll go away."

When they arrived at the resort, Allie realized Corliss was wearing his wedding ring. He noted her open-mouthed stare and smiled sheepishly. Fishing his wallet from his pocket, he showed her the circular impression in his leather wallet.

"I never stopped carrying it," he admitted.

"I guess I'll have to retrieve mine from my box," she said, still too stunned to notice what she was saying.

"What box?" he asked.

She wanted to bite her tongue. "My Corliss box," she reluctantly admitted.

He quirked an eyebrow at her. "You have a Corliss box?"

She nodded.

"What's in it?"

"My rings, some mementos, and some correspondence." Despite that she had tried to make it sound matter-of-fact and inconsequential, he smiled like the Cheshire cat and whistled appreciatively.

"You have a Corliss box. Who knew you were such a romantic? Can I maybe see it sometime?"

"Maybe," she said, turning to stare studiously out the window while he tried not to laugh. "Don't tease me, Corliss," she said huffily.

"I'm only laughing because *I* have an Allie box," he said.

That brought her up short. "You do? What's in it?"

"I'll show you mine if you show me yours," he said.

They arrived at the swanky hotel where he'd made the reservation. "Let's keep that policy in mind all weekend," she said, causing him to laugh so hard he ran into the curb when he tried to park the car.

The man watched through the telephoto lens of his camera, seething when he saw them laughing. They weren't supposed to be having fun, not when his life was teetering on the edge of disaster. His resentment grew, bordering on despair as he watched the husband get out of the car and open the door for his wife. Every loving touch, every smile, every private look was like a hammer blow to his psyche. How dare they? How dare they be in love when everything he had worked for was about to topple like a house of cards?

His finger twitched as it yearned for the trigger of his gun. One clean shot and it would all be over. But now wasn't the time; there were too many witnesses, and he was too exposed. The time was coming, though, when retribution would be meted. And next time, he silently vowed, his aim would be better.

CHAPTER 20

True to Corliss's prediction, they didn't see much of the idyllic little town on their weekend excursion. In their defense, theirs was a full-service resort with a restaurant, spa, golf course, and beautiful walking gardens. They spent a pleasant Sunday morning walking the estate before having brunch and playing a round of golf. Golf was something they had never done together, and the experience was a lot of fun.

The whole weekend was fun and refreshing. Allie felt like she hadn't stopped laughing since they left Chicago. The change of pace gave her confidence in their fledgling renewal, giving her hope that what was redeveloping between them was strong, strong enough to support the talk that was long overdue. She waited until they were home to broach the subject.

"Corliss," she began, but he interrupted her.

"You promised to show me your box," he blurted.

"I did no such thing," she said, distracted.

"You did so," he argued. "As long as I show you mine. It's not my fault mine is in Kentucky. I want to see yours."

She bit her lip, thinking. Obviously, he was trying to dodge a serious discussion again, but looking through her box might give

122

them the catalyst they needed. "Fine," she agreed. "You can see my box."

He carried their bags to their apartment and set them in their room before plopping on the bed. "I'm ready," he said.

She stood on her toes, peering up at the top shelf of the closet to reach her box.

"That's your box?" he said. "I've passed by that thing dozens of times and never knew it was anything significant. I thought it would be snazzier than plain cardboard."

"Remind me to decorate it for you," she said. "Is your Allie box lit with neon?"

"No, but it's shaped like a heart," he said. She quirked an eyebrow at him. "It was on sale," he added, blushing faintly when she laughed at him.

She lay beside him on the bed, the box between them. "Let's start at the beginning," she said as she sifted the box, lifting the lid so only she could see inside.

"Don't hold back," he said. "Show me everything. This is a fascinating glimpse into your mind."

"All in good time," she told him, smiling as she withdrew the first item.

"A stick?" he said, sounding disappointed.

"This is a very important stick," she informed him. "On the day we met, you walked me to my door. I was desperately hoping you'd kiss me—little did I know it would take six years," she said in an aside, rolling her eyes. "Anyway, I was standing there, expectant and nervous, when you bent and lifted my foot. You said, 'I thought you were walking like a horse with a burr in his hoof. There's a stick in your shoe.' You removed the stick from between the treads of my shoe and dropped it into my hand."

"And you kept it?" he asked, puzzled.

"It was the first thing you ever gave me," she defended. "And I thought your turn of phrase was cute when you compared me to a horse. Later I would realize that horses were your frame of reference for everything, like the time you told me I was as pretty as a speckled foal."

"I was wrong about that," he said. "You're as pretty as our best racing mares." He wagged his eyebrows at her, and she laughed. "What's next in the box? A gum wrapper? Used tissue?"

"The first picture of us together," she said, withdrawing a photo.

He took it from her and stared at it with a fond smile. "I was so crazy in love with you, and trying so hard to hide it," he said.

"Me, too," she said.

"When did you ever try to hide it?" he asked. "I think your most oft-repeated phrase was 'Kiss me, Corliss, please?'"

She jabbed his waist with her finger and he flinched. "It's a sign of my devotion that I withstood your rejection so long," she said.

"And it's a sign of my devotion that I held out so long; you were too young to trifle with. I took a lot of cold showers back then."

"Me, too," she said, making him laugh again.

They sifted through the box slowly, peeling away the layers of their relationship, laughing and smiling over old times, and occasionally kissing over some remembered romantic scene. He almost looked a little misty-eyed when he learned she had saved the pop tab he'd proposed with. She pulled out her wedding and engagement rings, intending to put them on, but he held her back.

"I'll do it," he said. Slowly, he slipped them on her hand, engagement ring first, then he kissed her. The kiss would have led to something more, but he stopped midway and grabbed his jaw, grimacing when the wires pulled too tight.

"Did I mention how much I hate having a broken jaw?" he muttered.

She gave his cheek a light, sympathetic pat before returning her attention to the box. And then she stopped short, staring at it.

"What?" he asked. "What could possibly be left in there? It's like Mary Poppins' bag—endless."

"There's one thing left," she said, beginning to doubt the wisdom of her decision to share everything.

"What is it?" he asked, still sounding jovial.

She bit her lip and slowly withdrew the christening gown, setting it on the bed between them. Corliss stared at it, blinking rapidly as his smile slowly fled. "Where did you get this?" he asked tightly.

"I found it in the hall closet after you left. I figured you must have bought it."

He nodded. "I bought it for you, for when you started feeling better about things. It was the last one the store had and I..." He trailed off and frowned. "Why did you keep this, Allie?"

She swallowed. How to explain? Where to start? "I kept it because it meant a lot to me," she said slowly.

"Why would this," he thumped the garment with his hand, "mean anything to you?"

"Corliss, that day, the day you picked me up at the doctor, things didn't happen the way you thought."

He looked up at her, perplexed. His silence was encouragement to keep going.

"I began cramping when I was in class. I was frantic. I found that doctor, but by the time I reached him, it was over. I had miscarried. The procedure in question was to remove pieces of the placenta that were lodged in my uterus. I would never have..." She shook her head. "Never. I would never do that to you or to our child, no matter how upset I was."

She wasn't sure what she had been expecting, but she was still surprised by his anger.

"What are you saying?" Then, not giving her time to answer, he plowed ahead. "Are you saying that for the past five years you've let me think you aborted our child? That you've willingly let me believe a lie? That you let me accuse you and walk out that door when all you had to do was tell me it wasn't true?"

"No...I...Corliss, I can explain," she said, feeling frantic all over again.

"How? How can you possibly explain any of this?" He shot to his feet and began pacing around the small space that was left beside the huge bed. "Allie, this is, this is so...How could you?" He stopped short and stared at her, accusation and anger and pain so vivid in his eyes she wanted to crawl away and hide.

"Please let me try to explain, Corliss," she said, sounding as desperate as she felt.

He didn't sit, but neither did he leave. Instead he stared at her, and she took that as encouragement to continue.

"That time was a horrible blur. I was in so much pain, physically and mentally. I was confused, and I felt horribly guilty and ashamed."

"If you didn't do anything wrong, then why did you feel guilty and ashamed?" he asked, his tone suspicious.

"Because I lost our baby, and I hadn't wanted it at first. I thought I was being punished. And I felt ashamed because I couldn't do what so many other women do as easily as breathing. What was wrong with me that I miscarried? I spent days, weeks, and months going over every minute of my pregnancy, trying to figure out what went wrong. Eventually I joined a miscarriage support group and learned I wasn't alone in feeling that way. Guilt is a common feeling after a miscarriage." She bit her lip and looked up at him, her eyes round and wounded.

He breathed in and out heavily for a few minutes, sounding as if he'd run a race and was trying to get oxygen into his overtaxed system. And then at last he spoke. "I can understand why you felt that way in the beginning. But that was five years ago, Allie. If at any time you had picked up the phone or come to visit, you could simply have told me what happened and it would have been over."

"Would it, Corliss? Can you honestly say you wouldn't have still been upset with me over my career and my reluctance to have kids?"

"I don't know, but at least I wouldn't have thought you went behind my back and got rid of our child."

"Why did you think that in the first place?" she asked. Gaining some anger of her own, she shot to her feet and crossed her arms protectively over her chest. "How could you ever think that, Corliss? Don't you know me at all?"

"You know exactly how it looked, and after everything that you said, how was I supposed to think anything different?" he yelled.

"Because you've known me since I was sixteen. How could you think so little of me?"

"Easily, at the time. Do you know how often you told me you wished you weren't pregnant? Do you know how much it hurt that you put your career ahead of me, ahead of our family?"

"I knew you resented my job," she yelled.

"Only when it became your first priority," he yelled. "Which it always was; which it still is. I've been here every day of the last two weeks, Allie, and I'm still trying to fit myself into your schedule."

"That's not fair, Corliss. You dropped back into my life with no warning, and you expect me to instantly re-shape everything around you. I have a life here."

"And I have a life in Kentucky."

They squared off, facing each other over the wide expanse of the bed, huffing like two steam engines after a long haul. Finally, he turned and stormed from the room, slamming the door behind him. Allie gathered up everything that had been spilled from the box, tossing it haphazardly inside before slamming the lid and shoving it back on her top shelf. So he was leaving again. It was nothing less than what she expected. Well, fine. She had survived for five years without him; she could survive another fifty.

She yanked open the drawer that held her nightgowns when he stepped back into the room, wearing his boxers. She turned to look at him in angry dismay. He frowned when he saw her expression.

"I'm not sleeping on that tiny couch," he said, jabbing his finger toward the living room. "Sleep there if you want, but I'm staying right here."

"I'm not sleeping there," she said, also pointing toward the living room. "I have court tomorrow, and I'm not showing up with a stiff neck." She ripped off her clothes and threw on her gown, angrily tossing her used clothes into the hamper before jerking up the covers on the bed and crawling inside.

He didn't say goodnight. There was no kiss, and he didn't reach a toe over his side to touch her. *But at least he's here,* was her last sleepy thought, and then she fell asleep.

CHAPTER 21

The jangling of the phone disturbed Allie from an already restless sleep. She reached for the phone at the same time as Corliss. His body covered hers like the world's heaviest blanket, but she somehow still managed to grab the phone first.

"Hello," she said groggily, squinting at the clock. Who would be calling at five in the morning?

"Allison," Marlin said, sounding groggy yet cheerful. "We found Pamela Pratt."

She sat up, shoving aside Corliss who had fallen back asleep on top of her. "You did? Where?"

"Joliet. A farmer found her in his field. She's pretty far gone, so we'll have to do DNA on her, but it's her; I'm certain of it."

"Her husband has family in Joliet," Allie said excitedly. In her head, her case was reshaping itself. Now she didn't have a missing person's case; she had a murder case with an actual body.

Marlin chuckled. "Yeah, he's in big trouble. I wanted to call you as soon as possible so you could file the appropriate motions to recess the trial until we get the body tested. Also I didn't know if you wanted to come to the scene today. We're going to be here awhile."

"Yes, definitely," she said. "I'll be there as soon as I can, and you're right about the motions. I'm going have my paralegal draft them now so I can be there as soon as possible. I don't want to miss a minute of this. That jerk is going to get what's coming to him if it's the last thing I do."

Marlin chuckled again. "Thatta girl. See you soon."

"You want some coffee?" she asked before he could disconnect. Who knew how long he had been up?

"Coffee sounds great. Thanks, Allison."

"No, Marlin, thank you. You're a lifesaver or, should I say, a case saver. There's no way Mr. Pratt is going to walk free now." Smiling, she disconnected, then looked at Corliss, her smile slipping. Part of her was tempted to leave. But she knew he would be frantic if he woke and she was gone. She could leave him a note, but that didn't feel right either. Reluctantly, she shook his shoulder. "Corliss."

"Baby," he murmured, reaching for her with a sleepy half smile. He snuggled her close, absently kissing whatever he could reach.

"Awesome timing," she mumbled sarcastically, squirming out of his reach. "Corliss, wake up," she said impatiently, shaking him again.

"Hmm," he said, still smiling at her as he began to stir. "What is it, sugar?" he threw his arm over her waist, closing his eyes again.

"Corliss," she yelled.

This time he sat up in alarm, frantically sweeping the dark room with his gaze. "What? What is it? What's wrong?"

"I have to go to work."

"Now?" he asked, confused.

"Yes, now. They discovered Pamela Pratt's body, and I'm going to go the scene. First I need to stop by the office and leave some instructions for my paralegal. I'll be gone all day."

"I'm coming with you," he said. He wearily scrubbed at his face before throwing off the covers.

"You don't have to do this; I'll be fine." After their steaming row the night before, she would appreciate the space away from him.

"I'm coming with you," he said stubbornly.

"Fine," she said. "Suit yourself. It's going to be a long, boring day." She turned on her bedside lamp and began getting ready for the day, putting on clothes and gathering supplies. In addition to her briefcase, she would also need her emergency field supplies, the ones she rarely used because she was rarely in the field. After adding in a few necessities for Corliss, she was ready to go.

"Aren't we making coffee?" Corliss asked, sounding almost desperate for caffeine.

"We're buying it on the way; I promised Marlin I would bring him some."

"Super," Corliss said irritably, locking the door behind them as they left the apartment.

"Don't start," Allie snapped. "He's a colleague, and he's already been working for who knows how long, and he's bound to be exhausted."

"Aren't we all," Corliss said darkly.

Allie wanted to tell him to stay home if he was so tired, but she refrained. Obviously they were both cranky and in need of either more sleep or a whole lot of coffee. They remained silent as they drove to her office. It was dark and a bit creepy, but Allie would still never admit how thankful she was Corliss was with her.

When they went back to the car, she sighed impatiently as Corliss pulled out his mirror and checked underneath.

"Why are you still doing that?" she asked. When he didn't answer, she tried another question. "Why didn't you do it at our apartment?"

"Because the security is better at our apartment. This garage is much larger and there's no attendant and the lighting is bad. Plus it stands to reason that whoever wants to hurt you would do it in public."

She didn't follow his logic, but she was too tired and irritable to argue about it. There was a not-so-small part of her that felt like ripping the stupid mirror out of his hands and dashing it on the ground a few times until it shattered.

"We're all clear here," he said, opening the passenger door for her.

You think? she wanted to snap. They drove through a coffee place and ordered larges for themselves, as well as for Marlin, and a few extras for any other officers that might be on the scene. After a half dozen sips of his coffee, Corliss seemed to relax a little.

"Why are you going to a crime scene?" he asked, his tone neutral. "I thought prosecutors didn't do that."

"I don't usually. But sometimes for big cases I like to make an appearance so I can get a feel for the scene. It helps me when I'm preparing a closing." She hated to say the next part, but she felt the need to be honest. "Plus, Marlin invites me sometimes. He says someone who sees both sides of the process is automatically a better lawyer."

"Marlin has a lot of opinions," Corliss replied, his tone losing some of its neutrality.

"He does," Allie agreed. "Must be why we're friends. I seem to be drawn to strong men."

Corliss darted her a glance and rolled his eyes. She turned to the window with a slight smile. She wished he would magically get over his hurt and anger so they could get back on track once again.

The sun was peeping over the horizon when they arrived in Joliet. The crime scene wasn't hard to find; there were a half dozen marked cars scattered in front of a cornfield with police tape securing the area and a bevy of reporters queuing up for interviews. The scene was so crowded that Allie and Corliss had to park far away around a bend and hike to the scene. As they approached, the reporters stopped what they were doing and scrutinized them with narrowed eyes. Were they important? Would they do an interview?

Before any could make up their minds and approach, however, Allie and Corliss were safely behind the tape and making their way to the center of the scene. The smell hit Allie before she saw the body. She withdrew mentholated rub from her bag and swiped it under her nose, offering some to Corliss who looked at it in puzzlement, not understanding its use. She mimicked wiping it under her nose and he shook his head, wisely turning to look at the horizon instead of at the crime scene.

Allie wished she didn't have to look, but she did. Viewing victim photos was gruesome enough, but nothing compared to reality. In addition to the stench, there was the fact that animals had been feasting on the body, rendering it into pieces and making off with chunks of flesh. All that remained of her skin was her scalp, covered with what had once been long dark hair. Now her once-beautiful mane looked like a grotesque Halloween wig. Allie swallowed down her revulsion, taking a bracing swig of coffee and trying hard to focus on the brew's pungent taste and aroma. She handed Marlin his coffee as he came to stand beside her.

"You're sure this is her?" Allie asked. The remnants bore no resemblance to the woman Pamela Pratt had been, at least not to her, but Marlin had more experience viewing dead bodies and trying to reconstruct their identities.

"Yep," Marlin said, taking a swig of his coffee. "Besides the resemblance, there's the fact that she was found with her identification and jewelry."

"Nothing missing from her wallet?" Allie asked.

"Not a thing," Marlin said.

Outsiders wouldn't understand how anyone could smile smugly while standing over a dead woman, but Allie's mind wasn't on the victim; it was on the woman's husband, and one more brick had been added to the case she was building against him. Robbery had been eliminated as a motive.

"Does this property belong to his family?" Allie asked, scanning the horizon.

"No, but he grew up down the road. I'll see if we can pin down some neighbors who remember him playing here as a kid," Marlin said.

Allie's smile grew wider. Marlin was the type of cop who liked to see the bad guys convicted. He approached cases from her point of view, always doing whatever he deemed necessary to help her win a case. They had a good working relationship, and she hoped someday he would learn to accept the situation with Corliss, that was, if they decided to stay in Chicago. She bit her lip and looked pensively at the remains on the ground, not seeing what was in front of her until she came to with a start and looked away with a shudder.

Marlin moved on, talking to the cops in charge of the scene. Since he was out of his jurisdiction, he was an official observer today, as was she. She pulled out her camera and began to shoot pictures. Hers wouldn't be the official crime scene photos, of course, but they would help her remember things she wanted to include in court. In many ways, writing a closing argument was much like writing a novel. She often had to set the scene and tell a story. Remembering the feel of an event helped her immensely. Even if she wasn't included in an active crime scene, she often went to one after it was cleared in order to look around and take pictures so she could get a feel for what had taken place.

Corliss moved to a stump, as far from the body as he could get, and sat looking out at the road. Allie took pity on him and fished around in her pack, plucking out his copy of *Oliver Twist*. He looked up in surprise when she dropped it in his lap.

"You brought a book for me?" he asked, sounding pleased.

"I warned you it's going to be a long, boring day. Might as well have something to do." Unable to resist the urge, she ruffled his hair, combing her fingers through his thick tresses, thinking it was unfair that a man should have such beautiful and thick hair.

As the day progressed, the scene became more chaotic. The media had caught a whiff of who the deceased was, and things were quickly turning into a circus. A large crowd of spectators hovered curiously on the other side of the tape, and more officers had to be called in for crowd control. For Allie, who had grown used to the cavalier disregard of Chicago, the small-town mentality of Joliet was jolting. Had she become calloused and jaded by her job? She hoped not.

Marlin tracked her down a few hours after she arrived. "Bad news, Allison. Your petition to have Pratt's bail revoked was granted, but he's flown the coop."

"He's gone?" she asked angrily. She had tried to get him remanded to custody during the trial, but without a body, the judge had granted bail.

Marlin nodded. "It's all over the news that this is Pamela Pratt. He's rabbitting."

"Well that's great," Allie said, so angry she wanted to kick something. When a conviction was practically in the hole, her suspect disappeared.

Corliss had apparently overheard the conversation because he approached with a frown. "Wait a minute, you mean that Pratt guy has been out of jail the whole time?"

Marlin turned away, refusing to even acknowledge that Corliss had spoken, but Allie turned toward him with a sigh. "I'm afraid so," she said.

"Why didn't you tell me?" Corliss said. "I thought if he was on trial, he was in jail."

"That's the way it's supposed to be," Allie said bitterly.

"Allie, this could be the guy who took a shot at you," Corliss said. He scanned the large crowd, drawing protectively closer to Allie.

"We've already established that it was Jimmy DeSant, and he's six feet under," Marlin said.

"You said you found stationary at his house. That doesn't mean he's the same person who shot at her," Corliss said.

Marlin rolled his eyes. "Do you have secret dreams of being a cop or something? Because, as you say in Kentucky, you're barking up the wrong tree. What's the likelihood of two psychos being after Allison at the same time?"

"Pretty good if you've made as many enemies as Allie has," Corliss said.

"This is ridiculous," Marlin said, growing more agitated by the second. "Allison, we're in the middle of a murder scene that's turned into a media circus. I can't have him here when I'm trying to focus on doing my job."

"I'm not leaving until Allie does," Corliss said belligerently.

The two men turned toward Allie, waiting for her to choose between them. She felt a headache coming on and yearned for more coffee, and that thought gave her a brilliant idea.

"Corliss, maybe you could run into town and grab us some food and some more coffee," she suggested.

"You want me to go?" Corliss asked. He tried to sound flippant, but she could see the hurt in his eyes.

"Yes, but I want you to come back," she said, causing Marlin to cluck his tongue in disapproval. "He's my ride," she told Marlin.

"I would be happy to drive you home," he said.

"I'm sure you would," Corliss said. "But I'm staying for as long as Allie wants me. What do you want for lunch?"

She checked her watch. "Is it lunchtime already?"

"Past," he said, smiling at her absentmindedness.

"I'm sorry; you must be starving," she said, giving his bicep a gentle squeeze.

"Do you think Joliet has any smoothie shops?" he asked, and she laughed. "You could come with me. Getting away for a few minutes might do you some good. It's bedlam here." He scanned the crowd with another frown. "And I don't like leaving you."

"What do you think is going to happen to her while she's surrounded by a dozen cops?" Marlin asked.

"Was I talking to you?" Corliss asked, glaring down at Marlin.

"I think I'll stay," Allie said, pretending nothing was amiss in their little trio. "The sooner I finish up here, the sooner we can go home." She wished Marlin would go away, but he made no move to leave. Deciding that soothing Corliss's feelings outweighed worrying about Marlin's, she stood on her toes and kissed Corliss's cheek. "Be careful."

"Yes ma'am," he said deferentially. He caught her hand and brought it to his lips, bestowing a kiss on the back of it. "And you do the same."

She watched him walk away, parting the crowd like a miracle worker as people made a path and then stared at him, taking in his height as well as the breadth of his shoulders. He turned the corner out of sight, and Allie once again focused on Marlin.

"Think the coroner is about done?" she asked.

"I think the coroner is milking things for the benefit of the cameras, but I'll see if I can nudge things alo..." His words were drowned out by the sound of an explosion, one that came from the exact location of Allie's car.

CHAPTER 22

Marlin tried unsuccessfully to hold Allie back, but she broke away as easily as she tore through the crowd of onlookers—like a hot knife slicing butter. The rational part of her brain told her she didn't want to see what she was about to see, but she couldn't not look. She had to see him, had to see Corliss and make sure he was really gone.

When she rounded the cornfield, though, all she could see was a twisted pile of burning metal. The fire was so hot she could feel the heat from where she stood a hundred feet away. She ran toward the car, knowing there was nothing she could do, but desperate to do something, and that's when she literally tripped over Corliss. She put her hands down, slamming them hard into the dirt in order to avoid landing on his already-injured body. She righted herself, frantically inspecting him. There were soot marks on his face and the wound on his shoulder was once again bleeding, but otherwise he looked intact.

"Corliss," she said desperately. She sank beside him and began smoothing her hands over him, feeling for injury, while a uniformed officer ran up beside her and began talking into his lapel microphone.

"I'm calling the ambulance that's here for the body ma'am," he informed her. "They're going to divert and take him." He paused. "Is he still alive?"

Allie looked up with a start. Corliss wasn't dead, was he? He didn't seem dead, but she hadn't actually checked for a pulse. She did so, pressing her hand to his carotid artery and practically crying with relief when she felt an answering beat in her fingertips.

The ambulance arrived almost as soon as she and the officer stopped speaking. Allie stood back, helplessly wringing her hands while the medics stabilized his neck and loaded him onto the gurney. Seeing the neck brace gave her a whole new set of concerns. What if he was paralyzed? How had he ended up so far away if the car was set to explode when he opened the door? Had he used his mirror to check for a bomb? These were questions only Corliss could answer, and he showed no signs of waking up.

Allie tumbled into the ambulance after the medics loaded Corliss inside. She sat on one gurney, staring at Corliss while the medics took his vital signs. She wanted to ask them how he was, if he was going to make it, but she was afraid of the answer. How could he survive whatever had happened to him? And, for that matter, what had happened to him?

Arriving at the hospital increased her anxiety because she had to let him go. She stood watching him with the sinking feeling that it might be for the last time. When she found the waiting room, Marlin was there, pacing anxiously back and forth.

"How are you?" he asked.

She tried not to be irritated by the fact that he had asked after her wellbeing when she was perfectly fine. At least he was here, and that was comforting. It would have been worse to be in a town far away, afraid, and alone.

"I need to make some phone calls," she said, although really she only had to make one call. She dialed Brent, hating to impart the bad news, but realizing the brothers would need to know everything as soon as possible. But as soon as she heard her brother-in-law's familiar drawl, she couldn't say a word; she was crying too hard.

❧

Corliss was having a wonderful dream. Allie was in his arms, and he was happy. For some reason, they were floating, but his arms still felt pinned by her weight. He came awake slowly, blinking as the last vestiges of the pleasant dream faded away, only the feelings didn't fade away. He still felt happy—euphorically so —and his arms still felt lead heavy. He tried to lift his head to look down at them, but couldn't. But his eyes were open, weren't they? When he tried to speak, his tongue felt stuck to the roof of his mouth, but one thing was true: Allie was there.

"You're awake," she said. She was perched on the side of the bed. She leaned forward, her palms coming to rest on either side of his head so she could inspect him. "And you need a shave. Big surprise. I swear you grow hair like kudzu."

At least, that was what he thought she said. It was hard to tell over the horrible ringing noise in his ears. "What happened?" he asked.

Allie laughed. "You're yelling. The doctor said you might have some trouble with your hearing."

"Huh?"

She repeated herself and, to him, it seemed she was speaking in a normal voice, but he could tell by the strain in her vocal cords that she was yelling. "You have a concussion, a very bad one. There was an explosion." She arched an eyebrow at him in question, waiting for him to remember.

"Oh," he said. "Right." He remembered the explosion now, mostly.

"What happened?" she asked, smoothing her hand gently over his forehead. He closed his eyes and leaned into her touch, like a puppy that was starved for affection. Her hand felt so cool and gentle against his overheated, aching brow.

"I almost opened the door without looking because you weren't with me. Something made me look, instinct maybe, and I saw the bomb on the driver's side. I was backing away when it went off."

"It went off before you opened the door?"

He nodded and winced. "It happens sometimes. There's a tubular incendiary device with the explosives at one end. When the door opens, the explosives rush to the other end, connect with a wick, and complete the circuit. Sometimes they can shift on their own. Head hurts." He didn't think his head had ever hurt so badly before. It felt like one of those big drums from high school marching band, the kind that was pounded with a heavy mallet. Every beat of his heart brought a renewed thump of pain. The ringing in his ears was driving him crazy. In fact, the only part of him that didn't hurt was his jaw. He ran his hands gently over the lower portion of his face.

"That's the good news. When they scanned you, they found your bones were healed enough to remove your wires. You're free."

Maybe later the news would make him happy. Right now it made him frustrated. He had sworn as soon as he was free, he would give Allie a proper kiss, and now kissing was the last thing on his aching mind.

"I'm going to click some more pain meds into your IV," Allie said. She picked up the little device that ran between his arm and the bag beside him and clicked it a few times. A few seconds later, Corliss's pain began to ebb. Unfortunately, unbidden sleep also began to steal over him.

"Call my brothers," he murmured while he was still conscious.

"I already did," Allie said, smoothing her hand over him again.

"They'll protect you," he added groggily.

"They're not coming for me, silly; they're coming for you."

"No, they'll know what to do," he told her, and then he fell asleep.

Allie heard them before she saw them. Actually, she heard people murmuring in the hallways, shuffling aside to make room for them. She hadn't realized the sound of a cluster of Honeywells approaching was so familiar until she heard it again. How many times had she lain in the loft of the barn, listening for the heavy scuffle of their feet on the barn floor? And how many times she peered down from the loft and watched them walk into the room as they did now, strong, capable, and in charge.

Their eyes slid over their brother, somehow assured he was okay even though he was unconscious, and fastened protectively on Allie.

"How you doing, sugar?" Brent asked.

In answer, she once again burst into tears. She hadn't cried since she last talked to him a few hours ago when she had been frantic, not knowing if Corliss would live or die. Now she knew that, except for a raging headache, he was going to be okay, and she was falling apart again. What was it about these brothers that made her act like such a, well, such a girl? Most of the world saw her as a capable, strong, and independent woman, but show her a Honeywell and she turned into a quivering mass of estrogen. Maybe it was a biological response to their overload of testosterone. Whatever the reason, she didn't resist when Brent came forward and hugged her as Everett dug in his pocket and handed her a handkerchief.

"There, now," Brent said, giving her a reassuring pat on her head. "It takes more than a bomb to take down a Honeywell."

The statement was so absurd she laughed, grinding her palms into her eyes. Good thing she had left the house too early for mascara this morning, or she would probably look like a raccoon. She might already due to the lateness of the hour and the emotional upheaval of the day.

"Let's get you home," Brent continued.

She bit her lip and looked at Corliss. "I don't want to leave him. I'll give you my key and you all can go home."

Brent shook his head. As the oldest brother, he was usually the official spokesperson for the group. "We talked to his doctor on our way in here, and he's going to sleep for a long time. You need to get some rest. We'll come back first thing tomorrow." When she still looked like she was going to resist, he gave her shoulders a squeeze. "This is what he wants; he wants you to be safe and taken care of."

Allie stopped resisting then because she knew what he said was true. Hadn't Corliss said as much during the brief time he had been conscious? She crept to the bed and pressed a gentle and lingering kiss to his lips. "I love you," she whispered, but in his drug-induced state, he didn't stir.

As they exited the hospital, the brothers formed a circle around Allie, blocking her from all sides so she was invisible between them. She wanted to protest, to say she didn't need their overreaching protection, but she was too exhausted. The drive to her apartment from Joliet was long. The brothers had to be as exhausted as she since they were on Kentucky time, had flown a few hours, and driven an hour to get her.

"You guys can have the bed," Allie said when they arrived home. "It's huge; I think it will fit all of you."

She didn't understand their looks of horror until Darcy spoke. "Men don't share beds, sweetheart, not even brothers. We'll sleep out here on the floor. You take the bed and get some good rest."

She scanned the circle of brothers, thinking how very much she had missed them. To the casual observer, they were all exactly alike, despite their height differences. But Allie knew better. The differences were subtle, but they were there. Brent, the oldest, felt the weight of responsibility deeply, always trying to think what was best for everyone else. He wasn't one to analyze feelings, his or anyone else's, but he was sweet, thoughtful, and generous.

Corliss was more analytical and thoughtful. He liked to daydream as much as he liked to read. Whip smart, he had achieved nearly perfect grades in school.

Darcy was the most suave of the brothers. He was also the most aware of his appearance and status in the community. Hardly a snob by anyone's standards, he still had an appreciation for the finer things, preferring to dress slightly better than his brothers and only date women who had as much wealth and status as he did.

At 6'11", Everett was the tallest brother, and also the quietest. He was a gentle giant, caring and tenderhearted. Most people mistook his quietness for stupidity, but they were wrong. Everett was an observer who enjoyed nothing better than people watching.

Grant was the stereotypical little brother. Even though he was older than Allie by a year, she had trouble thinking of him that way.

Rash, naïve, and happy-go-lucky, he was always ready for fun or trouble.

"I'm glad to see you guys," Allie said tremulously, an understatement if there ever was one.

"You're our family, sugar, and we're yours," Brent said.

She gave them a quavering smile and darted into the bedroom before she could burst into tears again.

CHAPTER 23

*T*he next morning was another early wake up, provided by another phone call from Marlin.

"A couple of witnesses spotted Pratt at the scene yesterday. If you okay it, we'll charge him with attempted murder," he said with no preamble as soon as she said a groggy hello. Since he sounded as exhausted as she felt, she couldn't fault him for being abrupt. With a crime scene turning into an attempted murder scene, his night had probably been long, crazy, and sleepless, especially because he had gone back there after sitting with her for over an hour at the hospital.

"I'll sign off on it," she said, pulling the receiver away from her mouth so she could yawn.

"Great. I'm going to put the word out with the media so we can turn up the heat on the elusive Mr. Pratt. I'll keep you informed."

"Thanks, Marlin," Allie said, yawning again.

Marlin chuckled. "Get some sleep, Allison."

"You, too," she told him. After a few fumbling attempts, she settled the receiver in its cradle, turning to face Corliss's side of the bed with a sigh. She missed him terribly. How had she gone five long years without him? Now after only one night alone, she felt bereft. She might have fallen asleep again if not for the sound of her brothers-in-law as they unsuccessfully tried to keep a low profile in the living room. Like Corliss, they were early risers.

"Morning, sugar," Brent greeted cheerfully when she emerged from her room. He stood in front of the coffeepot, unsuccessfully trying to figure out how it worked. She gently and wordlessly moved him aside as she made a large pot of coffee. She had the feeling they were all going to need it this morning. The brothers couldn't have slept well on the floor, with a single blanket and couch pillow for company.

"What's on the agenda for today?" Grant asked as Allie rooted around in her cupboards, looking for cereal that they would eat. Their taste buds ran as unhealthy as Corliss's.

"Court has been adjourned until I locate my suspect. I should go to the office, but I think I can phone it in today and have my paralegal put some things in order for me. That leaves visiting Corliss, unless there's something you guys want or need to do."

"We go where you go," Everett informed her. He easily reached over her head, setting out five mugs.

"You really don't have to," Allie said. "Mr. Pratt's picture is about to be splashed all over the news. I can't believe he would be stupid enough to try and take me out again right now." Then again, she wouldn't have thought him stupid enough to return to the scene of his crime and try to take her out there, either. Had she misjudged him? She had classified him as a cheating husband with a violent temper, but what if he was more? How did he go from a guy who killed his wife in a fit of rage to a man who designed a bomb and planted it on her car with a crowd of witnesses around the corner? What if he was simply a raging lunatic? Something didn't fit, and she was too tired to figure out what it was. There was something niggling in the back of her mind, but what?

Since there were only two seats in the small kitchen, she and the brothers stood around drinking coffee, eating cereal and bagels, and reminiscing over old times. The laughter and distraction they provided felt like a soothing balm to her overworked emotions. As soon as it was a reasonable hour, they took turns in the bathroom. At last they were all ready to go, but as she reached the door, her phone rang.

It was her landline, but Marlin had used that number the last couple of times he called. Thinking it might be him, she held up her finger to indicate she would be a minute and answered the phone.

"Is this Allison Miller?"

"Honeywell," Allie answered vaguely.

"What?"

"It's Miller-Honeywell. How can I help you?" Her brow puckered with impatience. *Get on with the sales pitch so I can tell you no and hang up the phone.*

"I didn't blow up your car."

She gripped the phone tighter. "Mr. Pratt?"

"That's right, and I didn't have anything to do with blowing up your car."

"Witnesses saw you at the scene," she said.

"They're lying. Why would I go there? I'm not an idiot." He hissed a breath through his teeth. "Look, I'm ready to come in, but I don't want to do it until I have your assurance that I won't be charged with attempted murder."

"I can't…" she began, but he interrupted her.

"Meet with me and talk to me and you'll understand what I'm telling you. I had nothing to do with it. I wouldn't know the first thing about building a bomb."

She rolled her eyes. As if she would ever meet with him. Hang a sign around her neck and call her "stupid."

"You can bring that officer friend of yours," he added. "The one who always sits behind you in court. We'll talk and you can look into my face and know I'm telling the truth, and then he can bring me in. I'll let him pat me down before we have the conversation."

Allie sighed, thinking. "I'll talk to Officer Hayes and get his opinion. What's your number?" He rattled off his cell phone number and she programmed it into her phone, deciding to call Marlin on the way to the hospital.

"Trouble, sugar?" Brent asked.

"That was the man who is accused of blowing up my car. He says he didn't do it."

"Don't they all?" Brent asked with a smile.

"Yes," she said, biting her lip.

"But you believe him," Brent guessed.

"I don't know," she said slowly. "But it's never really fit. What motive would he have had to do something like that in the middle of a crime scene, *his* crime scene? It would have made more sense if he blew up the scene, thereby obliterating any evidence." She began thinking about motive. Who had the greatest motive to kill her? That was when the elusive something that had been niggling in the back of her mind finally clicked into place. She stopped short, laying her hand on Brent's forearm and looking up at him in astonishment.

"What is it?" he asked.

"I know who's been trying to kill me, I know why, and I also know what I'm going to do about it," she said.

"You've had a productive morning, and you haven't even reached the car yet," Brent drawled.

Allie laughed as he held out a hand to help her into the SUV. "I didn't get a chance to ask you yesterday about Haley. Have you found her yet?"

Now it was his turn to sigh. "No. It's like she's disappeared off the face of the earth."

"Don't stop looking," she encouraged. "If you really love her, then don't give up on her."

"I won't," Brent promised. "Every day this ache inside me gets worse; I've got to find her so I can fill it up again."

She nodded sympathetically, knowing exactly what he meant. She had functioned without Corliss, but never at a hundred percent. Now the missing piece of her heart had returned, and she planned to keep it there. All she had to do now was catch a killer, and she faced forward, formulating a plan.

CHAPTER 24

"I'm surprised, Allison."

It was the third time Marlin had made the statement. The other two times Allie had responded with a shrug, but now she tried to explain her actions. "He said he wants to meet. He said he'll let you bring him in. I figured this was the easiest way of killing two birds with one stone."

"It's not only that," Marlin replied. "I'm surprised you would leave your husband in the hospital to do this."

"Corliss understands that my job isn't exactly conventional, that sometimes it has to trump family obligations."

Marlin snorted. "I wish my wife had understood that; we still might be married."

Allie hadn't known he was ever married, but now wasn't the time to discuss it. They stepped from his car and walked to the place where yesterday her car exploded. The car was gone, and now there was a barren scorch mark, surrounded by rows of corn. The scene had been cleared, the spectators were long gone, and now the place was eerily deserted.

"This is an odd meeting place," Marlin remarked with a frown. "I don't like it." They walked to the edge of the tall cornfield and waited.

Since it was late summer, the corn was fully grown and still green. Wind whipped through the stalks, creating an odd keening sound that did nothing to dispel the eeriness of the atmosphere.

"Who are the witnesses?" Allie asked.

"Hmm?" Marlin said absently as he scanned the area with narrowed eyes, waiting for Tyler Pratt.

"The witnesses. You said there were two witnesses who saw Tyler Pratt here yesterday. What are their names?"

"I don't remember."

"I suppose I can look at their statements later this afternoon," Allie said.

"I haven't gotten their official statements yet, but I have their contact information."

"Maybe when we're done here, we can stop and talk to them," Allie said.

Marlin stopped looking around. Instead, he turned to face her. "What's this about, Allison?" he asked suspiciously.

"It's about getting to the truth. There were no witnesses, were there, Marlin?"

"What are you talking about?" he asked.

"I'm talking about the fact that you made up witnesses to place Tyler Pratt on the scene yesterday, knowing he was a convenient way to shift blame for the bomb, like you dumped stationary at Jimmy DeSant's house to implicate him in the letters."

He laughed uncomfortably. "I think your brain is a little fried today. That's crazy. Why would any of that be true?"

"Because the bomb wasn't on the passenger side," Allie said.

"What?" Marlin asked. He ran his hand through his hair, disheveling it at the roots.

"The person who had been threatening me had also been watching me. He saw me with Corliss at least twice. He saw me in the passenger seat. He would know that when we're together, Corliss always drives, yet the bomb had been placed on the driver's side. And then I started thinking about the day we were shot at. Corliss is a foot taller than me, and he had been standing a few feet away. Yet the bullet hit *him*.

Unless someone was an insanely bad shot—and who would attempt to shoot someone if they were such a bad shot—then the bullet hadn't been meant for me; it had been meant for Corliss all along, as had the bomb. And, while there are lots of people who want to kill me, there's only one who wants to kill Corliss: you."

Marlin laughed uncomfortably again and shook his head. "Allison, this is crazy. I'll admit I was a little jealous of the guy, but you're talking about murder. Why would I do that?"

"Why, indeed? Yet you're the one who insisted on looking into the letters, approaching me about them as soon as I received the first one. I had only told Bunny about it, and I assumed she told you, but I checked; she didn't."

He licked his lips nervously. "Word spreads. I heard about the letters and decided to check on you because we're friends."

She shook her head. "Bunny told no one, she's adamant about that. You sent the letters because you knew we would spend exponentially more time together after that, trying to figure out where they came from. Then Corliss arrived and threw a cog in your plans."

"What plans?" he asked.

"I thought you always came to hear my cases because you had a keen interest in the law, but you had a keen interest in me, isn't that right, Marlin?"

"Look, I'm not on the witness stand here," Marlin said uncomfortably.

"You found any excuse necessary to work late with me, bringing supper, showing up at my house unannounced with new information we had to go over. I thought you were simply being a good cop, but you weren't; you were being a creepy stalker, and I refused to believe it, not even when my husband pointed out your unusual interest in me."

"He's not your husband," Marlin exploded. "A guy who abandons you and stays away for five years is not your husband."

"You don't know the story, you don't know what happened," she said defensively.

"Yes I do. I know about the baby. I saw your medical records."

Her jaw dropped. By accessing her medical records, he had broken quite a few laws.

"That guy got you pregnant and then abandoned you the day after you had a miscarriage. I would never do that to you. I would always be here for you. He deserved to die for what he did to you, for coming back and ruining everything that's between us." His eyes turned pleading, but Allie shook her head.

"You're sick," she said softly.

"Allison, it doesn't have to be like this. We can be together. Tell him it's over, and we'll forget anything ever happened."

"Did you kill Jimmy DeSant?"

"What?" he asked, confused by the apparent change in topic.

"Did you kill Jimmy DeSant?" she repeated slowly.

"Of course not. Jimmy's number was up when he started skimming the mob."

"Did you kill the judge?"

His eyes bugged. "Why would I kill a judge? That's crazy."

"Then all you're on the hook for is Corliss's attempted murder. If you plead, then I'll recommend a light sentence with mandatory counseling," she said. She thought the offer was generous, but Marlin looked thunderously angry.

"What? I'm trying to help you, and you want to put me away?"

"Marlin, trying to kill my husband, the man I love, the man I've loved for half my life, isn't helping me. It's insanity, and you need help."

So fast his hand was a blur, he drew his gun on her. "No, you need help. This ends today."

"How do you think you're going to get away with this?" she asked.

"Tyler Pratt showed up. We struggled. He grabbed my gun and shot you. When I checked on you, he ran away. I'll track him down and kill him later to keep him silent."

She shook her head. "Won't work, Marlin. Tyler Pratt is in custody. We talked this morning, and he's satisfied that I believe he didn't try to kill Corliss. His alibi is airtight."

He licked his lips nervously. "I'll figure something out," he said.

"I don't think so," Brent said, stepping through the corn with Corliss's gun leveled at Marlin's head.

"You're going to want to take the gun off our baby sister-in-law," Darcy said, stepping through on Marlin's other side with Allie's gun in his hand.

"I don't have a gun, but I would gladly pound your face in," Grant said, following his brothers.

Everett merely remained silent and intimidating, towering over the gathered group.

Marlin's hand dropped limply to his side. Everett reached forward and plucked the gun from his grasp.

"Wh-wh-wh…" Marlin stammered, looking around at the group of assembled Honeywells. Allie forgot how much they all looked alike to an outsider. She wondered if Marlin thought he was having some sort of mental break where he thought he was seeing four of Corliss.

"Did you get your recording, sweetheart?" Darcy asked. He took Marlin's handcuffs from his waist and used them to secure Marlin's hands behind his back while Marlin loudly protested.

"I did," Allie said. "Thank you."

"C'mon," Grant said. "Let's drop this guy off so we can go tell Corliss what we've been up to."

All the brothers had been uncomfortable with keeping the plan a secret from Corliss. They had left him, saying merely that they were taking Allie to work. Corliss hadn't said anything, but Allie knew he had been hurt and angry that she was leaving him to go to work. Now she knew he was going to be even angrier when he found out the danger she had willingly put herself in.

"It was the only way," she said desperately. "You'll tell him it was the only way, won't you?" she pled, looking around at all the others.

"Well, now, sugar, have you ever known us to give our opinion on anything?" Brent asked. "No, sir, we remain neutral and objective; that's our creed."

Allie laughed, easing some of the tension from her chest. "I've heard that about you Honeywells. You're easygoing."

"Low maintenance, too," Darcy said, although Allie wasn't sure if he was teasing. Their perceptions of themselves didn't always match others' perceptions of them.

Three of the brothers drove Marlin in his car while Brent and Allie rode in the other. They drove to Marlin's precinct, and Allie led the way while Marlin screamed for help and the brothers walked sedately beside him, nudging him in the right direction when he repeatedly tried to stop.

Since it was Marlin's precinct, and since he was a good cop who was also well liked, it took awhile for Allie to explain the situation. She had to replay the recording she had made several times before the light began to dawn and Marlin's coworkers understood what was going on. Allie's boss was called to the scene, as was Marlin's. By the time Allie and the Honeywells were free to leave, it was late at night, well past visiting hours at the hospital.

"Where are we going?" Allie asked when Brent bypassed the turn for her apartment.

"The hospital," Brent said.

"But visiting hours are over," she said.

"Those are a suggestion. It'll be fine, you'll see."

And she did. With the four Honeywells escorting her, no one stopped her or told her to go away. They waited outside the room while Allie went in, and then they retreated to the waiting room.

Corliss turned brooding eyes on Allie. "Did you get your work done?" he asked sullenly.

"Yes I did," she said. She went forward and kissed him until he responded, pulling her close and enjoying the fact that there were no wires restricting his movement. "I missed you today," she said when the kiss was over.

"Why did you go?" he asked. "I thought you were taking the day off."

"About that," she said, biting her lip. "There's, uh, something I have to tell you." Nervously, she launched into her narrative.

Down the hall in the waiting room, the brothers sat looking at magazines. They were far enough away that they shouldn't have been able to hear anything from their brother's room, but it was as if he was standing beside them when he yelled, "You did what?!"

"Now seems like a good time for coffee," Brent said. The other brothers nodded in agreement and escaped to the cafeteria until Corliss cooled down.

CHAPTER 25

Two days later, Corliss was released from the hospital. And he was still angry. To Allie's great annoyance, he wasn't angry at his brothers. No, all of his irritation was directed at her.

"They were doing what you told them," he said when she pointed out the fact that they were equally guilty in her little scheme. She rolled her eyes, secretly wondering if Corliss loved his brothers more than he loved her, and feeling petty for thinking such a thing in the first place.

The ringing in his ears had subsided to a soft buzz. His head still hurt, and his brain felt loose every time he turned his head. For that reason, he stayed in bed for a couple of days after he came home from the hospital, the first time he had ever stayed inert for so long in his life. That was why, when he finally started feeling better, he was filled with boundless energy. When Allie left for work on the third morning after he returned from the hospital, he cleaned the apartment, attacking all the hidden areas that hadn't been touched in awhile. He also cooked a nice meal, but he still felt restless. Reading didn't provide him with the same joy as usual. Allie watched as he paced nervously back and forth in their tiny living room.

"I don't know what's wrong with me," he said.

"I do," she said, closing the book she had been enjoying. "You're bored."

"I suppose," he said listlessly. He stopped in front of the bookshelf and brushed at some imaginary dust.

"Corliss," Allie called.

"Hmm," he said, still staring blindly at the books. Allie really had an abominable selection on her shelves. He would have to fill them with his own books, the sooner, the better.

"It's time for you to go home," Allie said.

He whirled to look at her, slamming his eyelids closed when the room spun. "What? What are you saying?"

"I'm saying I want you to go home to Kentucky. You're like a wild bird in a cage here. You're bored and restless and ready to get back to work. Not to mention the fact that your family needs you."

He scowled at her. "And you don't need me any more, is that what you're trying to say? Now that the danger is passed, I can go back to Kentucky like nothing ever happened."

She closed her book and set it aside, staring up at him. "Yes, that's what I'm trying to say. I don't need you to protect me anymore."

His scowl deepened. Why did her words sound like a question, as if she were waiting on him to say something? What was he supposed to say now? "Fine," he said tentatively. "I'll leave in the morning."

"Fine," she said. She picked up her book and began to read again.

So that was how they were going to play it. They were going to be cool and civilized this time, giving no hint of what was between them. Well two could play at that game. He selected some book from her idiotic collection and began reading, not realizing she was crying until his anger subsided. He glanced at her, watching fat tears plop onto the pages in front of her, and his heart melted.

He tossed his book aside, took hers, and tossed it aside, too. "Why are you crying?" he asked, sliding his arms around her.

"Why do you think?" she said, burrowing her face in the hollow of his neck. "You're going to go to Kentucky and miss everything."

"Miss what?"

"The baby."

He froze, gripping her biceps.

"That's right," she said angrily. "I'm pregnant."

He swallowed hard. She was pregnant, and she was upset about it. Again. "Just have the baby and I'll take it to Kentucky."

She jerked out of his embrace. "You're not taking my baby anywhere."

He blinked at her in confusion, trying to remember if pregnancy had made her nonsensical the first time, too. "What?"

"You heard me. You're not taking my baby, Corliss Honeywell. Either get on board, or butt out."

"What are you talking about?" he said. "You want the baby?"

"Of course I want the baby. Why do you think I got pregnant?"

"You got pregnant on purpose?"

"Well of course I did, Corliss. Why else do you think I haven't mentioned birth control since you've been here? Did you think I forgot? Do you think I would forget something that monumental unless it was on purpose?"

He blinked at her, trying to figure out if he was supposed to answer any of those questions.

She jerked farther out of his embrace, putting more distance between them on the couch. "And now you're going back to Kentucky."

"You told me to go back to Kentucky," he said, exasperated. "Didn't you mean it?"

"Of course I meant it," she said, crying harder now.

"Then what…"

"You're supposed to ask me to go with you," she yelled.

He blinked at her once again. "But you love your job here. You love your life. You would resent me if I dragged you back to Kentucky."

"Why don't you let me decide what I do and don't resent," she said, sniffling and wiping her nose. "You have no trouble browbeating me into everything else you want me to do, yet you won't do it when it comes to my job. I'm so tired of you tiptoeing around my career I could scream."

"I was trying to be sensitive," he said, becoming angry.

"Well, stop it. I'm your wife, and I'm carrying your child. Demand that I go back to Kentucky with you and find a job there."

Did she really mean that? He was confused, and confusion made him angry. Maybe it would help if he cleared the air a little where she was concerned. Tentatively, he reached out to take her hand. He had never been afraid of Allie before, but he had never seen her like this. "Allie, I love you. You're my wife, and I want to be with you. I don't want to take you away from a life you love. But it would be like a dream come true if you actually wanted to return to Kentucky with me."

"Oh, Corliss," Allie said. She burst into renewed and violent weeping before throwing herself at him. Corliss flinched, not sure at first if she was attacking him. When he realized she was simply crying, he lifted her, settling her into his lap.

"That was so sweet," Allie said, at least he thought that was what she said. It was difficult to tell with her face pressed to his chest. She lifted tear wet cheeks to look at him. "Of course I want to go to Kentucky. It's our home. I never intended to practice in Chicago."

"But..." he started. She interrupted him by pressing her fingers to his lips.

"Let's not rehash the past."

He hadn't been intending to rehash the past, only to try and understand the present. If it was hormones making her act so crazy, then he figured that was a good sign. He was sure she hadn't been this crazy last time she was pregnant, though he wisely refrained from saying as much to her.

"It's going to take me a few weeks to tie up my job here, though not as long since Mr. Pratt pled guilty to his wife's murder. You can go back to Kentucky, and I'll join you when I can."

He shook his head. "I'm not leaving you." In her present state, he didn't trust her not to get into a street brawl with the next person who looked at her cross-eyed.

"Okay," she said. Sighing happily, she rested her head on his chest. "I have a good feeling this pregnancy is going to turn out well. Things feel different this time."

"They sure do," he agreed, his tone still wary as he waited for her to have another mood swing and outburst. When he heard her soft, steady breathing a few seconds later, he realized she was asleep.

He carried her to their bedroom and deposited her on the bed, spreading out beside her to watch her with a smile. Somehow in the course of the last few days, his anger at her had evaporated completely. He wasn't sure it was gone for good, but he felt confident that when it came back, they would deal with it and move on. Maybe that's what marriage was all about, a series of highs and lows that a couple worked on together, no matter what. As he watched her sleep, so pretty, even with tears streaking her face, Corliss determined that no matter what, he wouldn't leave again. Allie was his wife, for better or worse, in crazy emotional outbursts or horrible misunderstandings. Bad times would come, but so would good, and they would face them together, always.

With that thought in mind, he closed his eyes and fell asleep, his arm securely around his wife.

Thank you for reading *Wild and Wounded,* the second book in the Honeywells of Kentucky series. For more books, please check out my website at www.vanessagraybartal.com